Captain Westwood's Inheritance

Lynda Dunwell

A Sweet Regency Romance

Romantic Reads Publishing

www.RomanticReadsPublishing.com

. . .

Captain Westwood's Inheritance
First published by Musa Publishing in the USA
February, 2013 in ebook format

This edition by Romantic Reads Publishing
Staffordshire, United Kingdom
Copyright © 2015 Lynda Dunwell

ISBN-13:978-1-910712-00-9

To my family and friends

ACKNOWLEDGMENTS

Thanks to the dedicated team at Romantic Reads
Publishing, especially editors Betty Turner, Maggie Glynn
and fellow author and beta reader Heidi McAnna.

Cover Design
SelfPubBookCovers.com/RavenandBlack

Other books by Lynda Dunwell

Regency Romances

Marrying the Admiral's Daughter
Colonel Weston's Wedding (2015)

Historical Romances

Tomorrow Belongs to Us: Titanic Series

Titanic Twelve Tales:
Short Story Anthology

Historical Crime/Romance

Josh Walker Investigates Novels:

What is Love's Sign?
The Mayor's Mistress (2015)
Death of an Artist (2015)

Chapter One

Portsmouth, August 1802

Jonathan stepped into the street, blinked, and raised his hand to shade his eyes from the mid-afternoon sun. Slowly he placed his captain's hat on his head, drew up to his full height, and wondered how much the landlord of the Blue Post Inn charged for bed and board since the Peace. He had but a few coins in his pocket. Dry-mouthed, he tried to swallow to quell the deep ache gripping his stomach. How could his father, a man he held in great respect, have gambled away his estates? But worse, even faced with ruin, how could his father have taken his own life?

"It's Captain Sir Jonathan Westwood is it not, or do my eyes deceive me?"

Surprised to be addressed by his title, Jonathan squinted at the small man who blocked his path. "I am Westwood, but forgive me sir, do I have your acquaintance?"

"Excuse the presumption, Sir Jonathan, do you not recognise me? I am Mr. Winters I have the living at Aston." He thrust his hand in the captain's direction.

Reeling from the bad news his banker had imparted, Jonathan paused for a few moments unsure of how to reply. Instinctively, he adopted the same ploy he used when called upon to rally his men before battle: suppress all private thoughts. "Of course, I do remember you sir, although I am surprised you recognised me for I was only a mid-shipman the last time I visited Aston Grange." He shook the parson's hand.

"It is a great pleasure to see you again, Sir Jonathan. The Peace has brought home many of His Britannic Majesty's finest officers and, of course, I include your good self among them."

"You flatter me sir, I am but one of '*We few, we happy few, we band of brothers.*'"

"You quote the Bard of Avon nobly sir," Mr. Winters' face stiffened. He removed his hat and fingered the brim in a circular motion. "My sincere condolences sir, regarding Sir Humphrey, we have, of course, offered prayers for him at the parish church but the nature of his demise...most unfortunate, you do understand?"

Jonathan hardly heard the cleric's words. A pain stung his insides as if he had been punched below the belt upon the mention of his father. "I've just had the news from Mr. Bayley, the banker." He coughed and removed his hat, "I knew my father took the carriage accident badly, and mourned the loss of my mother and brother. I...I have only made land today and planned to journey to the Grange, perhaps to find my father there. Now my arrangements must change."

"That is regrettable, Sir Jonathan, but Sir Humphrey hasn't lived on the estate these five years past, and so you would not have found him there. Aston Grange has seen a succession of tenants. The current gentleman is Captain Quentin, a naval officer of some renown. Perhaps you are acquainted with him?"

Jonathan shook his head, inwardly struggling to take in the news about the estate, which had been his father's favourite especially in summer. He swallowed deeply, as another annoying pain gripped his insides. "Captain Quentin? No sir, I have heard the name but we have not been introduced."

"Then perhaps you know another neighbour, Admiral Richmond of Witton Abbey?"

Jonathan welcomed the diversion it forced him to fight against his inner anguish. "I served under him as a midshipman but did not realise he had settled at the Abbey."

"He bought the estate when he retired from his naval duties. Unfortunately, he met with a hunting accident recently and suffered a broken leg, but it hasn't stopped him marrying a very fine lady from

3

Penley Court." Mr. Winters' face broke into a wide grin.

"Penley...of course, Lord Norton's estate. I remember my brother and I used to fish in the trout steam there." Happy memories of long summer days, running barefoot over meadow land and tickling trout in the cool stream sprang to mind. The recollection comforted him and his stomach ache eased.

"Admiral Richmond married Lady Mary Rufford, Lord Norton's sister. I had the privilege of conducting the service six weeks ago."

"Rufford? Captain Rufford's widow?"

"Yes sir, an admirable lady, if I might be so bold. She is very good to the poor. Mrs. Winters always speaks highly of her."

"I remember Lady Mary. She sailed with her husband for many years. I would welcome the opportunity to wish the couple happy."

"Then sir, forgive my boldness, but why not accompany us back to Aston this evening? You are most welcome to stay overnight at the parsonage and you could call upon the admiral tomorrow."

Jonathan thought for a few moments but couldn't see how he could prevail upon the parson's hospitality without feeling a measure of guilt. "Mr. Winters you are most kind, but I must go to London to investigate my father's...passing and settle his affairs."

"But Captain, the London mail coach has already departed, and surely you do not intend to start the journey on horseback, do you?"

Jonathan, still reeling from the tragic news, needed more details but rushing to London may not be his best course of action. "Sir, you are obviously well-acquainted with navy men. I have been at sea for six years. My equestrian skills are in my head, but I doubt if my back and legs could take the strain of a day's ride."

"Then stay at the parsonage at least overnight. You will be a most welcome guest, Sir Jonathan. At present, I have my sister's daughter as a guest, and would welcome male company at my table. Come to my aid sir, if only to usher the ladies away. Grant me the pleasure of enjoying a good glass of port with another gentleman. After dinner, we will be able to discuss matters in detail, something which we cannot do satisfactorily in Portsmouth High Street."

Jonathan saw Mr. Winters glance furtively along the street. What was troubling him?

"I beg of you sir, I would greatly welcome the opportunity to speak with you at length." Again he looked about him anxiously as men, delivery boys, and carters dodged each other, all plying their respective trades.

Jonathan considered the invitation but he could not impose on the parson for more than a night. "I would not want to burden you unduly, sir, but I would welcome any opportunity to uncover the truth about my father."

"Indeed sir, I understand, but as it was the admiral who related the news to me about Sir Humphrey, you must go to Witton Abbey and get the details from him direct."

Jonathan nodded his agreement and felt the pressure of a hand at his elbow as the parson drew him to one side.

"I feel you would be best advised to hear my account also, something I cannot impart here in the street. I am sure Captain Quentin will also assist you. Unfortunately he is visiting his father in Staffordshire with his new bride. Quentin recently married Admiral Richmond's daughter."

Anxious to be acquainted with all the particulars relating to the estate and his father, Jonathan nodded. "Sir, you have my measure. I will accept your invitation with gratitude."

* * * *

"My dear, you will not at a loss for fashion and style whilst you are with us at the parsonage." Mrs. Winters turned to her niece as if to import some great words of wisdom. "Portsmouth might be a naval port, but there is no lack of shops. Why, I have it on the very best authority that Lady Mary and Miss Richmond purchased the fabric for their wedding clothes from this very establishment." She pointed to a double bow windowed shop bearing the name Grey's Drapers over the central front door.

Catherine Ellis smiled and followed her aunt into the emporium. Two neatly dressed assistants greeted them cordially. Catherine glanced at the well-stocked shelves and smiled her approval. As a mill-owner's daughter she had the measure of quality cottons and muslins. She stood in silence for several moments admiring the interior of the establishment which proved a very welcome respite. After two days of her six week visit, she had begun to wonder if she could stand her aunt's constant twitter for the full duration of her stay. Mrs. Winters, a short, roundish figure, had scarce stopped to draw breath since they left the parsonage. Catherine opened her mouth to speak but she wasn't quick enough.

"I can't thank your mother enough for sending you to us. I wrote with all haste when the banns were read. Can you imagine the excitement in the neighbourhood?"

Again Catherine made to speak but only managed a monosyllable. "No—"

"A double wedding in the parish between the two most prominent families, ah, the joy!" Mrs. Winters smiled. "Of course, it was unfortunate you missed the ceremony, indeed Miss Richmond and the Admiral were considerably late, keeping Captain Quentin and Lady Mary waiting almost at the altar. Of course, Mr. Winters had to intervene and save Lady Mary the embarrassment of entering the church without the bridegroom. For my part, I let Lord and Lady Norton wait in my best parlour for what must have been a full half hour. Lady Mary was very patient and her brother and sister-in-law the most respectful of guests. Inviting them into the parsonage was the very least I could do. In confidence, my dear, because I know, like me you are the soul of discretion, there was a moment when I thought we may not have any weddings at all. Can you imagine the scandal that would have ensued?"

Catherine bit her lower lip, determined to keep her own counsel. Her mother had obviously not made all the facts clear to her sister-in-law when she had replied about the visit. Certainly her father hadn't mentioned her recent engagement when he accompanied her south from Liverpool. Also, she doubted if he had taken Mr. Winters into his confidence before he returned to the north. "No, Aunt Winters, I cannot possibly imagine a situation where a bride is jilted."

"Why, the entire county was filled with eager anticipation of the union between Miss Richmond and Captain Quentin. Of course, we all knew it was inevitable from the moment they met, but who would have thought Lady Mary and Admiral Richmond." She pointed to a length of apricot silk on the counter, removed her glove, and began testing the quality of the fabric between her finger and thumb.

"Miss Richmond, she is the admiral's daughter?"

"Yes, a very fine lady and I might say an exceedingly good friend of mine." She turned to the assistant. "Do you have something similar in pale green?"

The young man nodded, "If you will excuse me, Mrs. Winters, I will look in the stock room. We have just received a new delivery of the finest silks from Macclesfield."

Mrs. Winters smiled and turned back to Catherine. "Of course, when Mrs. Quentin returns from her honeymoon she will reside at Aston Grange. Although as Captain Quentin is only the tenant, I don't know long they will remain in the neighbourhood."

"And Lady Mary?"

"She has removed to Witton Abbey. It is a fine establishment although so is Penley Court, which belongs to her brother." Mrs. Winters adjusted the wide brim of her bonnet as she lifted a length of pale green ribbon closer to her eyes, then discarded it on the counter. "Should the earl have no requirement for the estate, who knows what will become of it? We may have a new tenant there before the autumn. So you see, my dear, the extent of our acquaintance in the neighbourhood. We are received by all the best families, as I told your mother."

Catherine turned to feel the quality of a bale of muslin sprig spread before her. "I do like this. The blue embroidered flowers are very pretty." She passed her fingers inside the double folded fabric and imagined it made up into gown perhaps trimmed with matching blue ribbon. It was the first time she had thought of dresses since she had left Liverpool.

"Then why not order a gown? Madam Irene's establishment is only across the street. She is one of the finest dressmakers outside of London. Mr. Winters informs me your father has been most generous with your allowance, and there is nothing like a new gown to bring a bloom to a girl's countenance."

"Am I in need of pleasantries?"

Mrs. Winters reached across the dressmaker's counter and touched her niece's forearm. "Yes, my dear, I believe you are."

* * * *

Catherine could not take her eyes off of the naval captain accompanying her uncle along the street towards them.

"Can you see who is with Mr. Winters?" Mrs. Winters tugged her niece's arm.

"A navy captain, aunt, but I do not know him."

"There are times when I wish I was taller."

Catherine kept her gaze firmly fixed on the officer, who made her uncle look very small as they walked along side-by-side. The captain's hat added several inches to his already tall and slender frame His gold braided epaulettes glistened in the afternoon sun as he strode slowly yet purposefully towards them. His appearance exuded command, his stance authority and his face—it was handsome. Catherine made a mental note of his features in order to sketch him when she returned to the parsonage. Her heartbeat quickened as the ill-matched pair of gentlemen drew closer. Mr. Winters lifted his cane in the air as if to signal to his wife and niece he was approaching with a valuable cargo in tow.

"My dear," a self-satisfied grin spread across the parson's face, "let me introduce Captain Sir Jonathan Westwood. You may recall he was staying with his family at the Grange when we first moved to the parish."

The captain removed his hat and made a slight bow.

Mrs. Winters replied with the customary bob. "I am delighted to renew our acquaintance Sir Jonathan. It has been many years since we had the pleasure of attending your parents at the Grange. Please accept my most sincere condolences on your tragic loss."

Catherine's opinion of her aunt changed as she listened to her speaking to Sir Jonathan. Aunt Winters could act without thought and speak incessantly. However, on this occasion, Aunt Winters' tactfulness over Sir Jonathan's bereavement was admirable.

"And this is Miss Ellis, my niece who is visiting from Lancashire," Mr. Winters said.

As the captain bowed his head, Catherine thought she saw deep sadness in his face. Dark smudges beneath his eyes made him look tired. His complexion was slightly browned from his life at sea, and tiny white lines creased the outer corners of his eyes. His features were most regular, his nose straight without being too long, his mouth generous, and he had thick eyebrows, which could have made him appear studious if he didn't have the longest eyelashes she had ever seen on a male face. With his dark broody looks, he could have been a poet rather than a naval officer. She made a demure curtsey in his direction and lowered her chin.

"Have you been in Hampshire long Miss Ellis?"

She lifted her head before replying. "No, Sir Jonathan, only two days, this is my first visit. I have never ventured so far south before."

"Miss Ellis and her father were due to travel overland, but since the Peace, they were able to take a packet from Liverpool," Mr. Winters said.

"How did you find your sea voyage?" the captain asked.

Catherine looked up into his dark brown eyes and found his scrutiny of her a little disturbing. However, she liked the tone of his mellow voice. "I thoroughly enjoyed my days at sea, although we scarce left sight of land. We enjoyed mild weather, fresh winds, and the voyage was far more comfortable than hours spent inside a coach. Unfortunately, my maid took sick as soon as we left harbour, but I am pleased to say neither my father nor I were afflicted."

"The malady can strike even the most experienced sailors, Miss Ellis. I am heartened that you enjoyed your voyage."

Mr. Winters stood in silence, his outstretched fingers pressed together as if in prayer. He turned to his wife, "My dear, I have invited Sir Jonathan to accompany us back to Aston. He would like to call upon Admiral Richmond before he journeys to London."

Mrs. Winters' face brightened. "I trust you will find a most hospitable welcome at the parsonage, Sir Jonathan."

Inwardly, Catherine smiled. The captain was the best looking naval officer she had ever seen, although there had not been a great proliferation of navy men in her part of Lancashire.

"I have business to attend to," Sir Jonathan said, "if you will excuse me. At what time will you be leaving Portsmouth?"

"Four o'clock," Mr. Winters replied, "then we shall have no difficulty making Aston in good light. We shall be at the White Horse Inn."

* * * *

"Is Sir Jonathan eligible?" Mrs. Winters asked her husband as they took some light refreshments at the inn where they had left their carriage and stabled the horses.

"As far as I am aware, my dear, he has been at sea for many years. Unless he has some pre-arrangement or family commitment, it is likely that he is unattached."

"You must ascertain his circumstances as soon as possible, Mr. Winters. As he is staying under our roof, I particularly wish to know."

"But—"

"You must discover his eligibility because we have Catherine staying, and it is vital we take advantage of every opportunity presented to us."

The parson let out a long sigh. "But my dear, he has just received news of the loss of his father and under the circumstances I—"

"Mr. Winters, Sir Jonathan is a navy officer ashore after years of service. It didn't take Miss Richmond long to fix Captain Quentin and do you not recall the crush at Lady Mary's summer ball? Why, half the county turned out to parade their daughters before the highly eligible Quentin." She shook her head, "No, I shall not be moved on this. We must encourage suitable suitors for Catherine whilst she is in our care. It is our duty."

Catherine sipped her tea, vexed that they spoke about her almost as if she wasn't there. Perhaps it was their way. They had no children of their own and as her aunt was now in her mid-forties, the chances of offspring must be becoming increasingly remote.

"Has Sir Jonathan inherited the Grange?" Mrs. Winters asked.

"As you know, my dear, Captain Quentin did want to purchase from Sir Humphrey but the circumstances surrounding ownership give much cause for concern. If the rumours I have heard are true, then Mr. Granville Richmond is the new owner. I might further remind you, whoever owns Aston Grange is also in possession of the gift of the living we currently enjoy. You have met the admiral's nephew and we have already found ourselves victims of his wild imagination. Sincerely, I hope true ownership will be established. The estate should remain with the Westwood family. As for Sir Jonathan, I shall accompany him tomorrow to the Abbey and see if the admiral can throw further light on the matter."

"Whatever you discover, Mr. Winters, I would be obliged to have immediate intelligence of all matters. Most likely Sir Jonathan will only be with us for one night. We must make a good impression upon him. And Mr. Winters, ensure you sit in the forward seat next to Sir Jonathan. I shall sit opposite with Catherine."

"I am diverted, madam, I thought you couldn't abide riding backwards. Haven't you always said so?"

"I don't like it, but I can tolerate it for a good cause," Mrs. Winters said.

"Good cause? I do not comprehend your meaning."

Catherine watched with mild amusement as her aunt rolled her eyes at her uncle, although she had no notion what her aunt's *good cause* might to be, either.

"I will sit opposite you, thus placing Sir Jonathan opposite Catherine. Then he will be able to observe her pretty face all the way back to Aston." She grinned.

Catherine felt her cheeks flush, from the moment she had arrived at the Aston parsonage with her father and maid, Mrs. Winters had launched into what was evidently a matrimonial campaign. But how much had her mother told Mr. and Mrs. Winters in her letter to them? But why was Aunt Winters doing this? Catherine pressed her lips together but couldn't stop thinking of Rossi. He had touched her heart, of that she had no doubt, but he had also deceived her. The experience of believing she had fallen in love and then to have her hopes of happiness shattered when his true marital status was unveiled, was cruel. Now it would take more than a smile from a handsome face to turn her head. She looked at her aunt. "I am sure a gentleman like the captain has far more important matters on his mind than to notice me."

Mr. Winters coughed. "I believe that is so, he needs time to mourn and is best left alone to do so. Also, Mrs. Winters be aware before you go marrying the captain off to any of the eligible young ladies in the neighbour, I suspect he is short of funds."

Mrs. Winters gasped her hand flying to her mouth. "But he has the title and Westwood House, not to mention any prize money he may have accrued at sea. No, husband, you are mistaken."

The reverend eyed his wife's face solemnly, "No madam, I am not. Sir Humphrey left considerable debt which the dutiful son must settle. I am told Westwood House is mortgaged and suspect Aston Grange will not be recovered easily by Sir Jonathan. If you must find him a wife, then ensure she has a fortune, or a well-heeled father who will pay a good sum for his daughter to call herself Lady Westwood."

Mrs. Winters frowned, "Oh, dear."

Catherine breathed a deep sigh of relief perhaps her aunt's conversation would be just tolerable during their return journey.

* * * *

Jonathan dropped the carter a few coins, as a couple of stable lads unloaded his sea chest at the White Horse Inn. To one side of the busy coaching yard, he spied a small carriage being made ready to leave. He assumed it belonged to Mr. Winters and sauntered towards it. He wasn't wrong.

"Sir Jonathan."

He wasn't sure who called his name. Although unused to being addressed by his title, he turned in the direction of the voice calling to him. It was Mr. Winters. Since meeting the parson, Jonathan had returned to the bank to negotiate a loan until he could reach London and see his agent. For the first time in his life, he owed money. The feeling did not sit well with him.

"Over here," Mr. Winters called, as he helped his wife and niece up into the carriage. With the ladies seated, Winters remained outside. "It is a privilege and pleasure to have you stay with us, Sir Jonathan. Please, take the seat at the far window."

"My pleasure," Jonathan said. He removed his hat and squeezed his large frame through the small door. "Good afternoon, ladies."

"Delighted to see you again, Sir Jonathan, I hope you have been able to conclude your business in Portsmouth to your satisfaction." Mrs. Winters said.

"Yes thank you, madam, I have." He manoeuvred his long legs into a comfortable position, trying to avoid nudging Miss Ellis. Almost as if she had read his predicament, she moved her knees to the side of the carriage out of his way. He looked directly into her dark brown eyes and said, "Much obliged, Miss Ellis."

Mr. Winters climbed aboard, sat down with great gusto, and grinned at his three companions. He tapped his cane on the roof of the carriage and the vehicle lurched forward. Soon they had left the bustle of the garrisoned town behind and were traversing the chalk Downs.

Jonathan looked out over Spithead for a final glimpse of his beloved sea. He had never seen so many ships laid up before, bobbing around, skeleton-like, their masts bare and yards denuded of sail. Their bare hulls reminded him of prison hulks, bursting at the seams with human cargo, yet bound for nowhere.

"Sir Jonathan, will you miss the sea?"Miss Ellis asked.

Jonathan turned his attention back to his travelling companions. "Indeed I shall, Miss Ellis. I went to sea aged fourteen and it has been my home for over twenty years. Ask any sailor and he will tell you the salt gets in our veins and sometimes we suffer land-sickness, in the same way the sea malady takes landlubbers."

Catherine smiled. "I mentioned my maid, Martha, earlier today. She has vowed never to go to sea again. I'm afraid, Uncle Winters, we shall have travel back to Lancashire by mail coach, when I return north."

"Goodness my dear, I could not allow a young lady, who is under my protection, and her maid to travel alone on the post." Mr. Winters said. Mrs. Winters nodded her agreement.

"Alas," Catherine sighed. "I have not received news confirming my father's safe return home yet. Although he did say he would call into Manchester on business. So, I might have to prevail upon your good self to accompany us, if my father cannot spare the time."

"But you have only just arrived." Mrs. Winters said, "You cannot be planning your return journey already."

"Of course not, aunt, but given the choice I would much prefer a sea voyage than travel overland. What is your opinion, Sir Jonathan?"

"Indeed, Miss Ellis, I am in complete agreement with you, however, I suspect I am somewhat biased." He had been looking at her for several minutes, trying to decide what she was thinking, or more importantly, what she thought of him. That surprised him. He hadn't been concerned with the personal thoughts of a young lady for how long? He couldn't remember. Perhaps he had been at sea too long and lost the delicate art of polite conversation. What would his mother have advised? *Encourage people to talk about themselves, people always like to do so, and listen.* "And how do you like Hampshire, Miss Ellis?"

"Admirably, Sir Jonathan, I especially like the light. Mornings seem clearer in the south to me, although I have only been here for two days, the weather has been fine and dry."

"Ah, the weather," Jonathan smiled, then remembering his mother's counsel asked, "Do you play and sing, Miss Ellis?"

Mrs. Winters straightened her back. "My niece is very competent at the pianoforte and she has a sweet voice. She is also a talented artist and has received instruction from a very fine Italian art master."

Miss Ellis' cheeks flamed a deep crimson. Was she embarrassed to have her talents praised, or was it the mention of the Italian art master that caused her discomfort? "Then I shall look forward to hearing you, Miss Ellis, and seeing your artwork."

Jonathan lent back against the squabs, folded his arms, and watched her closely. Was that a slight smile breaking at the corners of her small mouth? As the carriage rounded a bend, the sunlight fell on her face. She had fine dark eyebrows, dark eyes, a straight nose, not too long or too snub, and an unblemished complexion. Brown curls softened the sides of her face, which was surrounded by her blue velvet bonnet, trimmed inside with white pleated silk. She had a matching blue spencer over a white muslin gown. On first observation, Miss Ellis appeared to be a very attractive young lady and he wanted to know her better. The carriage lurched, almost as if to jolt him out of his daydream. Quickly he dismissed the idea. He had no business thinking about young ladies, especially those who would expect nothing short of a marriage proposal. He must push all such thoughts to the back of his mind until he could sort out the estates and get on an even keel financially. In the interim period he could only look and admire at a distance. Captain Sir Jonathan Westwood was not in any position to make a lady an offer of marriage. The carriage lurched again and shook him out of his daydream. Whatever could he have been thinking of?

* * * *

Attended by her maid, Catherine changed into her white muslin with the blue sprig for family supper that night.

"Do you wish me to dress your hair with blue ribbons, miss?"

"Yes, Martha, Mrs. Winters says I must look my best." Catherine sat before the glass at her dressing table.

"Sir Jonathan is a very fine figure of a man, especially in his captain's uniform. There was quite a bit of excitement in the kitchen when he stepped out of the carriage with Mr. and Mrs. Winters. Cook said, 'we'll have to prepare something a bit more special than the cold mutton Mrs. Winters ordered this morning.'" Martha giggled, "Folks hereabouts have a strange way of talking don't they miss?" She picked up pins from the tray, folded the blue ribbon and fixed the loops.

"I'm sure the local people say the same of Lancashire folk, Martha. So, we're to have a feast tonight, are we?"

"Yes miss, I don't know what cook has prepared because I had to help Sally turn down the bed and make-up the guest room. Sir Jonathan is very tall, isn't he, miss? Why, he had to duck to get through the door upstairs. I do hope he doesn't forget and hit his head."

Catherine giggled as the image of the handsome captain clutching a bruised brow flashed before her. "Sir Jonathan has lately commanded a warship and I don't think there's a great deal of headroom on board those vessels. I'm convinced he can cope with low ceilings and narrow doorways extremely well."

"Oh." She stooped to pick up the pin she had dropped. "I'm sorry, miss...but if I might be forward, will you be making drawings of the captain?"

"I might," Catherine paused, sensing Martha was cooking up some scheme or other. "Why do you ask?"

Sheepishly, Martha looked into the mirror. "Could I have one of your drawings of him?"

"Whatever for?"

"It was when we, that's Sally and me, saw him getting out of the carriage. Well, we both thought he was very dashing and...if I had a picture of him, well I could show everyone couldn't I? It's so much easier when you have a picture instead of trying to tell them what he looked like."

"Hmm...Martha Cope, are you developing a *tendre* for Mr. and Mrs. Winters' guest?"

"Oh, no miss, nothing of the sort, only I was thinking when we go home I'd like to show my mother and sisters."

Catherine thought for a few moments. "Are you home-sick?"

Martha stopped pinning hair. Her head fell forward, "A little," she said softly, "but I was glad of the opportunity you gave me to travel south and my mother's very pleased to receive the extra two shillings I'm earning as a personal maid."

"That is very well then, for I am grateful she was willing to let you come." Catherine glanced at the mirror, turning this way and that, very pleased with the developing hairstyle. "I cannot imagine how Miss Donaldson would have fared, had she come south with me. She is very precise, if a little old-fashioned, although my mother wouldn't have parted with her."

"She gave me a huge list of things I must and must not do and insisted we went through every one before we left."

"Did she? And are you using her list?"

"I would, miss, if I could, although Miss Donaldson assumed I would. Now I feel a guilty about it, as I didn't want to tell her I can't read or write."

"Do you wish to learn?" Catherine asked.

"Oh, yes, miss, it's the only way I'm going to get on in service, isn't it?"

Catherine nodded. "Then I will teach you."

"Begging your pardon, miss, but you couldn't teach me to speak French as well, could you, the way you and Mrs. Ellis speak?"

"Why do you want to learn?" Catherine asked curious to know the girl's motive.

"What if those Frenchies invade? They say that Boney wants to conquer England like he's done with other places. It might be useful to know what they're talking about if they do come here."

"Is that your real reason?" Catherine asked, amazed that her maid knew about Bonaparte.

Martha smiled into the mirror, "No, miss, but Miss Donaldson would be green with envy."

* * * *

Aston Parsonage appeared the same solid stone-faced building with a circular driveway that Jonathan remembered. He recalled his brother mentioning in his correspondence the extensive improvements to the house their father had sanctioned about ten years ago. He missed his brother's letters filled with news from home, comments about the political situation, and various projects the Westwood family had been pursuing. There was only one area missing from his brother's correspondence. There had never been a mention of a young lady. Of course, as the heir, there was always an expectation to marry and produce offspring, but Jonathan had never seen a hint of an engagement or possible marriage union. Now it was too late and that responsibility had come to rest on his shoulders.

The upper room Jonathan was given looked over the stable-yard where Mr. Winters kept his small carriage and horses. It was a modest establishment that befitted a man of the parson's standing. As he gazed over the yard, watched the lad groom the horses and lead them into their stalls, silently he thanked Mr. Winters for his hospitality. He shrugged off his naval coat and laid it carefully over the chair beside his hat. He stared at both items for several minutes. Would he wear them again in command of a vessel?

The question left a bitter taste in his mouth. He filled the bowl from the ewer, splashed cold water over his face, and dried his hands. He took a small key from his waist coat pocket and unlocked the paddock on his sea chest. The stalwart wooden box opened with a groan as Jonathan stared inside at the meagre contents. He had little more than his days as a mid-shipman, except his best dress uniform. He reached for the miniatures, swathed in linen, and unwrapped them one by one. Likenesses of his father, mother, and brother looked back at him, as they had always done. Kind faces, elegant in their youthful bloom as he wished to remember them.

He set them on the table before him, arranging them in order—father, mother, and brother. "I vow, as God is my witness, that I will not rest until I have restored the Westwood estates." He put his elbows on the table and let his head sink onto his hands. He had made the most important promise in his life and he had no idea of how he was going to accomplish it.

Chapter Two

Catherine completed several sketches of Sir Jonathan before she joined her aunt in the best parlour. Mrs. Winters insisted they use it because they had an eminent guest in the house. Catherine smiled, obviously her father, nor she, merited sufficient social stature to require the room's usage in the Winters' eyes as they had not been entertained there on their arrival at the parsonage. But tonight Mr. and Mrs. Winters were all politeness to their guest.

"Ah, Sir Jonathan, I did not recognise you in your brown coat," Mrs. Winters said as he entered the room. She pointed to the place next to her. "Won't you take a seat? Cook informs me we shall have to be patient if the fowl is to be roasted to perfection. I did intend us to have mutton this evening but no sooner had I crossed the threshold, I had to deal with a mighty commotion in the kitchen."

Catherine glanced quickly at her aunt. There had been no great disturbance when Mrs. Winters went to instruct cook—Catherine had heard every word. On the contrary, cook had been most helpful, but did remind her mistress that they only had two chickens and sea-faring gentlemen have the most fearsome of appetites.

"Mrs. Winters, I have no doubt you were able to steer your kitchen staff to calmer waters. As for my apparel, I am on the shore, so it is best I get used to my situation, besides I have no desire to draw attention to myself either here or in London."

"Very wise, Sir Jonathan," Mr. Winters nodded. He put his pen down on the writing slope he had open by the window and dusted the note he had written. Lifting the small sheet to his mouth, he blew the surplus grains of sand away. "I am sending to Witton Abbey, announcing your arrival in the neighbourhood and asking the admiral to receive us tomorrow morning." He folded the note, melted some sealing wax onto the edge of the paper, and pressed his seal into the dark red wax. He rang the bell and his manservant entered. "Take this to Admiral Richmond at Witton Abbey", he said, "and await a reply."

The servant duly acknowledged the request, collected the note, and left.

Whilst Mr. Winters had been writing and instructing his manservant, Catherine took the opportunity to observe Sir Jonathan in his country gentleman's attire. As he sat next to Mrs. Winters, Catherine thought he looked ill-at-ease. Perhaps it was the dull brown of his coat, or his plain cream breeches. she watched as he crossed his ankles, noting his shoes looked well-worn. A few moments later, he uncrossed his ankles and appeared uncertain of where to place his feet. Was he experiencing the same nerves that had afflicted her since he entered the room?

He sported a simple cravat, tied without pretension to the latest fashion. Indeed, Catherine had only seen the high collars and fancy waterfall tied cravats in illustrated magazines. Did real gentlemen actually wear them? She wanted to ask him about his naval exploits in the Caribbean, but the doors opened and a servant announced that dinner was ready to be served.

Sir Jonathan rose and offered his arm to Mrs. Winters. "Oh, Sir Jonathan, I couldn't possibly...perhaps...no."

"Go into dinner with Sir Jonathan," Mr. Winters urged his wife, "I shall escort my niece." He crossed the room and offered his arm to Catherine.

"Thank you, Uncle Winters," she smiled and together they paraded formally into the dining room. It wasn't a large room, but pleasantly situated with three tall windows looking onto the garden. Mr. and Mrs. Winters sat at opposite ends of the table and Catherine sat across from Sir Jonathan in the centre. The arrangement suited her because she could observe him at close quarters and add to her sketches of him later. Immediately she warmed to his dark brown eyes, noted the fine white lines at the far corners of his eyes, and found the sweep of his eyelashes mesmerising.

"I understand you have plans to go to London, Sir Jonathan?" she asked.

"Yes, Miss Ellis, once I have reacquainted myself with Admiral and Lady Mary Richmond, I shall be in London attending to my father's affairs. So, I regret my stay at the parsonage may only be brief."

"Then we must make the most of your company whilst you are with us, mustn't we Catherine?" Mrs. Winters said.

"Alas, my dear, I must press an earlier claim on our visitor's attention," Mr. Winters declared. "I have precious little male company in my house and have matters to discuss over my best port. So, when dinner is done, my dear, you must retire to the withdrawing room and leave us gentlemen to our business affairs."

Mrs. Winters' eyes narrowed as she looked along the table at her husband. A manservant brought the first course of soup into the room and placed it on the table. Mr. Winters then led a long prayer—so long Catherine feared the soup would be cold before they tasted it.

* * * *

Jonathan rose along with his host when the ladies left. Mr. Winters nodded to his manservant and two glasses of port were brought to the table. "That will be all," the parson said to his man.

Jonathan lifted the small glass to his lips, tasted the dark ruby-red liquid and was pleasantly surprised. "An exceedingly good vintage, Mr. Winters, if I am not mistaken." He raised his glass to his host.

"I've kept it special in my cellar," Mr. Winters whispered, beckoning him closer. Your father acquired a few barrels about twelve years ago. We were told not to ask questions and I have to confess, sir, I didn't. Sometimes a little knowledge can be most dangerous, do you not agree?" he chuckled.

"Indeed," Jonathan moved his chair closer to his host and sat down.

"Another?" Mr. Winters refilled the glasses and left the decanter on the table between them, "A cigar?"

Jonathan shook his head. "I've never taken to the habit, I used to be the butt of many a joke in the Caribbean, but I never had a taste for it. Not like your excellent port, sir."

"On that we are agreed. Why, I do believe, my cigars have mellowed in their box these past five or six years. I only kept them for Sir Humphrey."

At the mention of his father's name Jonathan's chest contracted. Throughout dinner, whilst engaged in small talk, he hadn't thought of him. Now his grief flooded back. He lowered his head for a few moments and took a deep breath. The smell of his father's tobacco seemed to haunt his senses. Recovering, he looked up, "Mr. Winters, there are matters you wish to discuss with me?"

"Yes, Sir Jonathan, and I do not wish these matters to reach Mrs. Winters' ears. My wife suffers with her nerves and distressing as this business is, I would wish to keep the news from her for as long as possible." He clasped his hands together on the table, intertwining his fingers as if in prayer.

Jonathan noted the change in his host's expression, the man was deeply troubled. "How can I help?"

"Today in Portsmouth, you were not the only man who visited Mr. Bayley at the bank, I too paid him my quarterly call. As you are aware I receive a stipend from Aston Grange and, indeed, my living and this parsonage is within the gift of that ancient estate. All of the monies have been withdrawn from the estate account on the order of London lawyers acting on behalf of the new owner, Mr. Granville Richmond. I was astounded, sir, that such action could have been done so swiftly, or that the bank allowed it."

"And this was the first you heard of this action?"

"No sir, I received a letter from the same lawyers but two days before. But with my brother-in-law expected that very day accompanying his daughter, I could hardly rush in haste to either Portsmouth or London to challenge the contents. I had to keep the letter to myself because of the seriousness of its consequences. And, of course, remain silent lest my wife should hear of it."

"What exactly is the problem? Lack of funds, surely, you have some reserves."

"Some, sir, but very little as I have been served notice to quit."

"But...I do not understand, surely you can apply to your bishop."

"I can, sir, but I doubt if I will find another living with such a comfortable abode or so kindly a neighbourhood. I have met the admiral's nephew, Mr. Granville Richmond, and my dealings with him have been far from satisfactory. Indeed, I know him to be deceitful and dishonest. His own uncle has banned him from Witton Abbey. Why he should want me out of the living, I can only imagine he plans to install his own man in my place, or Heaven forbid, deprive the good parishioners of Aston their right to attend divine service."

Jonathan thought for a few moments, when he returned home, he had no notion of the storm that awaited him. Earlier in Portsmouth, when he had called into the bank to ensure he had sufficient funds to finance his journey home to his father, he could not have imagined the squall he had stepped into. He drew consolation from the knowledge that he was alone in his destitution and hoped that his father's debts would not entirely deplete his accumulated prize money. But until he could reach his London agent, he could only estimate his own worth. Now, he realised others were suffering for his father's actions. The honour of his family name was being brought into question. He felt responsible for Mr. Winters and did not see why he was being treated so cruelly by Mr. Granville Richmond.

* * * *

"Whatever can the gentlemen be talking about?" Mrs. Winters asked.

"I have no idea," Catherine said. "Shall I play or would you prefer a game of cards?"

Her aunt let out a long sigh, "I have no head for the card table, I can never remember which cards have passed or even which ones I need despite holding them in front of me. Please play something cheerful, Catherine. Oh, dear, the coffee has gone cold I shall have to send for fresh when the gentlemen eventually join us."

Catherine sat at the small pianoforte in the corner of the drawing room, selected a simple country dance tune, and began playing. Mrs. Winters followed her and stood close by.

"Mr. Winters plans to visit the admiral tomorrow with Sir Jonathan, I have asked him if we might accompany him, but he refused. I do not know what has come over him of late. It would be the perfect opportunity to introduce you to Lady Mary, I told him, but did he listen? No, he was adamant that only he and Sir Jonathan went to the Abbey."

Catherine continued to play, it was a familiar tune and she hardly needed the music. "Perhaps if the weather continues to be fine I might walk around the village. I would like to take my sketch book, the countryside is so different from Lancashire, I'd like to capture some of it to show mama when I return home. Miss Cope could accompany me."

"Well as Sir Jonathan will not be with us and *we* are not allowed to visit the Abbey, there seems little else you can do. However, perhaps if you were to take the path towards Witton Abbey—"

She didn't finish. At the sound of male voices in the hall, she rushed across the room and sank onto a sofa chair. "Carry on playing Catherine we must appear totally at ease."

As the gentlemen entered, Catherine played Mozart. She liked the interwoven pattern of his compositions. From her seat behind the instrument, she had a clear view of Sir Jonathan as he entered and felt a tingle of anticipation grip her insides, similar to the reaction she had felt throughout dinner. She had noticed that Sir Jonathan took only a limited portion of chicken and did not load his plate with vegetables, whereas her uncle tucked into his large meal with relish. Mrs. Winters had twittered on about the weather, the fine shops in Portsmouth, the two dresses Catherine had ordered from Madam Irene, and several other insignificant topics that Catherine could no longer recall.

She looked up at Sir Jonathan, who stood adjacent to the pianoforte. "Do you play?" she asked.

"A little," he replied, "my brother and I were taught by my mother, who was most accomplished. However, it has been years since these hands have touched the ivories, I doubt if I could put three notes together."

Catherine continued to play, "I think you underestimate your talent, sir, for it is my belief that a skill developed in childhood remains throughout life."

"Upon that we are in agreement, but some skills require regular practice to ensure they are ready for use when called upon. I have been at sea for six years with only the occasional foot on land. The chance of hearing a piano played was rare, as to actually playing myself?" He shook his head. "However, it is a pleasure to hear some Mozart again."

"Did you receive instruction on another instrument, perhaps?"

"Alas, no, but it might have served me better if I had. There are some accomplished musicians in the service who were regularly called upon to entertain the officers and, of course, below deck the men entertained themselves with sea shanties and jigs."

Catherine smiled and began playing "Heart of Oak". She glanced up into Sir Jonathan's eyes and her heart lurched. Quickly she looked down at the keys, anxious not to make a mistake as she was playing from memory. As she approached the chorus, she played louder.

"*Heart of Oak are our ships, Jolly tars are our men*," he sang in a clear tenor voice, completing the chorus and second verse.

"Bravo!" Mr. Winters applauded when the captain had finished.

"Bravo, indeed," Catherine said, clapping her hands together. "You have a fine voice, sir."

"What a perfect duet you make," Mrs. Winters said, "I hope there will be other occasions when we shall hear you playing and singing together. Why, I am in such a flutter. My heart swells to hear such a fine song in praise of our glorious navy."

"Alas, my dear, the Admiralty does not share your sentiment, otherwise we would not find ourselves at peace with our enemies and half the British fleet laid up in port. Admiral Richmond, a man I hold in the highest respect, often laments the situation." Mr. Winters looked at Sir Jonathan, "Will you return to sea if war breaks out again? The admiral believes Bonaparte will not be content until he rules the world."

Catherine noticed a wave of sadness in Sir Jonathan's face. Was he thinking of his future or the terrible news he had received earlier in the day? She tried to imagine life without her parents, especially her mother, but the thought was too painful. She pushed it to the back of her mind. Rossi had tried to persuade her to run away with him. He had promised her an artistic life in London once they had eloped to Scotland. It hadn't occurred to her that such a marriage might separate her for life from the parents and home she loved. Until Rossi's deception was exposed. The sound of Sir Jonathan's voice snapped her out of melancholy.

"I am a sailor. If my country needs me, then I shall go to her defence. Whether the Admiralty will grant me a ship is another matter."

"Catherine," Mrs. Winters called, "will you delight us with a song?"

* * * *

Catherine stretched her limbs, sat up in bed, and thought of two men: Rossi and Westwood. She had slept well and been dreaming. Usually she didn't remember her dreams, but this time the men had so vividly invaded her slumber.

Rossi, dark and mysterious with his wavy hair flopping over his Roman face, deep set brown eyes, heavy brows, and generous mouth. She had drawn him numerous times and knew his every feature by heart. Sometimes she had deliberately made his overlarge nose smaller, experimenting with his features, trying to discover if she could make him appear handsome. But it was his flamboyant mannerisms, his passion for his art, and his beautiful accented voice rather than his looks that had touched her heart. Rossi was so different from any other man she had met in their circle in Lancashire. How she had enjoyed the art lessons under his watchful and critical eye, his surly brooding looks, and how he said her soft words lifted him from his solitary world.

Westwood, or perhaps she should call him Sir Jonathan? Strangely, in her dream he had been plain Westwood. Tall and commanding, his dark and somewhat unruly hair was tied in a sailor's pig-tail. Perhaps the fashion for shorter hair hadn't reached the service yet. Mr. Winters said Sir Jonathan planned to go to London. Maybe there he would acquire a more fashionable style? But what did she know of London fashions? Except from the illustrations she had seen in magazines and the reports brought back to Lancashire by neighbours who had been fortunate enough to visit town. Mr. Ellis had always refused his permission for her and her mother to go to London.

"Manchester or Liverpool is far enough for any northern lass to venture," Mr. Ellis said whenever a trip south was mentioned. But she yearned to go to the metropolis, not to shop at the numerous warehouses and clothing emporiums, but to view the art exhibitions and galleries.

Sir Jonathan had shown interest in her work and she hoped there would be an opportunity to show him some of her sketches and water colour paintings. However, whether he had an opinion about art, she had no idea, but it was kind of him to take an interest in her work.

It must have been early, for there were few sounds coming from the house as she pulled a cashmere shawl over her nightdress, picked up her sketch book and charcoals, and padded to the window seat. She drew back the curtain and took in the morning view. Mist clung to the hill behind the parsonage and the garden glistened with dew. In the yard, below her window, a stable boy tended a horse. She sat down, drew her knees up to support her sketch book and began drawing the scene.

As she outlined the animal's sturdy frame, Sir Jonathan strode across the yard, stopped, and spoke to the stable boy. Catherine froze as a tingling sensation starting in her belly wound its way the length of her backbone. Her shoulders tensed. Would he see her if he chanced to look up? She leaned to the side of the window, attempting to make herself smaller but really to get a better view of the captain. But was he a serving captain? She didn't know. He wore the same brown coat and cream breeches as last night. The lad pointed down the road, and Sir Jonathan strode away in the given direction.

Catherine followed his every stride until he disappeared around a curve in the lane. She looked down at her sketch and held it at arms' length to view. Dissatisfied with it, she flipped back a few pages to yesterday's unfinished portraits. Her heartbeat quickened. The quality of the drawing was far superior to her early morning effort. Could that be because they were all the same subject? She dismissed the notion but, nevertheless, started a new sketch of Sir Jonathan.

Chapter Three

Jonathan felt a wave of nostalgia sweep over him as the Winters' carriage turned into the entrance of Witton Abbey estate. As they approached the gates, the keeper emerged from his cottage, with a small boy at his side.

"Hold the horses," the driver called as he pulled on the straps and brought the carriage to a stop. The gatekeeper sent his lad to the horses' heads. "Good morning, Mr. Winters," he said doffing his cap to the parson, a bunch of keys jangling at his belt.

Mr. Winters leant out of the carriage window. "The admiral is expecting us. I'm accompanied by Sir Jonathan Westwood."

"Aye, I'd been told to expect you gentlemen."

From the other window, Jonathan watched him unlock the gates and wave the carriage through. "I don't ever remember the Witton gates shut when we used to visit," he said.

"And they didn't used to be, until late," Mr. Winters moaned, "but since the Peace you wouldn't believe what has befallen the countryside. Men need work, too many are on shore and there isn't sufficient employment for them on land. Captain Quentin staffs the Grange with his old crew and the admiral has taken on more agricultural labourers than he really needs, especially if they are men who served with him. But it's the highwaymen. We are not safe. Several carriages have been held up by Frenchies, yes sir, it seems since the Peace French pirates can roam the countryside at will."

Jonathan lifted an eyebrow in surprise. He had taken the parson for a man of reason, however, prone to exaggeration at times. He had no reason to doubt his word, but French pirates? Surely the parson was misinformed.

As they descended from the carriage, Jonathan looked up at the old ivy clad building. A survivor of the dissolution of the monasteries in Tudor times, the frontage had been rebuilt into something more acceptable to Georgian architectural tastes in the latter half of the last century. He remembered it as a welcoming and comfortable establishment. Under Admiral Richmond's ownership he expected it to be orderly, well-managed, and thriving.

"Good morning, Sir Jonathan, Mr. Winters," said the butler. "Admiral Richmond received your note, Mr. Winters and will receive you in the library."

"Thank you Middleton," Mr. Winters nodded.

"This way, please gentlemen, if you would care to leave your hats?"

The hallway through which the butler conducted them was familiar to Jonathan, but the paintings displayed on the walls had changed. In his boyhood, there had been a gallery of long faces, these had been replaced with seascapes and ships. There was also a ship's bell and a sand-timer.

"The admiral likes to keep ship's time," Winters said in an authoritative voice.

"Very wise," Jonathan nodded.

When they entered the library and Middleton announced them, Admiral Richmond remained seated in an armchair. "Can't stand for long on this infernal leg," he said, "but you are most welcome Sir Jonathan, why it must be twelve years at the very least." He held out his hand to Jonathan, who crossed the room and took it.

"Admiral Richmond, sir, a pleasure to see you again."

The admiral turned to his wife, who had risen. "My dear, you remember Westwood?"

Lady Mary greeted him formally with a slight bob. "Good morning, Sir Jonathan, it's a pleasure to renew our acquaintance and please accept our condolences."

"Thank you Lady Mary," Jonathan said, bowing his head slightly.

"Mr. Winters, I hope you are well?" she asked.

"Yes, I and Mrs. Winters are in good health. At present we have a visitor at the parsonage, my niece, my sister's child down from Lancashire. Her name is Miss Ellis. May I or my wife introduce her to you?"

"Of course, please ask Mrs. Winters to bring her for tea one afternoon soon."

"Thank you, Lady Mary, you are most kind."

"Yes, well now we have attended to the niceties, we have serious matters to discuss," the admiral said, "be seated gentlemen."

Mr. Winters and Jonathan hesitated, Lady Mary was still standing, they looked at her anxiously, expecting her to leave.

"Sit down, my dear, then these gentlemen can take the weight off their feet." He glanced up at Jonathan, "Lady Mary has my confidence, besides she knows as much of these offences as I do and I welcome her advice."

Lady Mary turned to her husband, smiled and sat in the chair next to his. She touched his sleeve, briefly, and mouthed. "Thank you."

"Have you seen this notice, Mr. Winters?" The admiral waved a copy of the *London Gazette* at the parson.

"No sir. Should I have?"

"Yes sir, I quote: To be sold by auction the next presentation to a most valuable living in the county of Hampshire. The vicinity affords the best coursing, also excellent fishing, extensive cover for game etcetera. The surrounding country is beautiful and healthy and the society elegant and fashionable. The agents are Hoggart and Phillips of London, and before you ask, I have made enquires, the advowson of Aston Parish is for sale, sir, your living?"

Mr. Winters paled. "I had received a notice to quit a few days ago and have brought the letter with me. I am very worried that I shall be cast out of my home and living. What am I to do? I cannot tell Mrs. Winters." He drew the letter from his pocket and offered it to the admiral.

Admiral Richmond frowned and took the letter. Quickly he scanned the contents and handed it to his wife. "Read this Mary."

She picked up her spectacles from her sewing table nearby, put them on and read the letter.

"I think Mrs. Winters is the very least of your worries, sir," the admiral said as he turned to Jonathan. "Can I assume Mr. Winters has outlined the particulars of your father's death?"

"Yes, sir, as related to him by you. Hence, I must to go London to settle his affairs as best I can. Although, I understand my father faced financial ruin, knowing the man, I cannot believe he took his own life." Jonathan noted the look that passed between the admiral and his wife as he spoke.

"Neither do we," the admiral said. "The weight of responsibility for this insidious matter rests heavily upon my shoulders. I had vowed not to speak my nephew's name in his household after his actions. I am most distressed that my neighbours are suffering the consequences of his actions. The time has come to act. Mr. Winters, I will endeavour to purchase the living, however, I shall have to use agents. I cannot see my nephew willingly selling me the incorporeal hereditament but I will do everything in my power to secure it. I cannot see you chased out of your home and calling by my villainous nephew."

"Oh, Admiral Richmond, I am quite overcome by your generosity. I feel humbled, sir, to have your friendship," Mr. Winters said, his tone quite emotional. "But my direction has come from lawyers, how do I know they are acting on Mr. Richmond's behalf?"

"Who else?" the admiral barked. Lady Mary had finished reading the letter and whispered to her husband. The admiral nodded. "I shall also approach Lord Norton, as the owner of Penley he might also wish to take an interest in the parish living."

Whilst the admiral was talking, Middleton had entered the library. He signalled to the admiral, who beckoned the butler to his side to deliver his message. The admiral looked at his guests, "Bagshot, yeoman farmer on the far side of Aston Hill, has taken a turn for the worse and wishes to make his peace with his Maker. Mr. Winters, one of the Bagshot sons is outside requesting you accompany him back to the farm house. Apparently, Bagshot has not yet made his will."

Mr. Winters leapt to his feet. "Then I must about my calling, if you will excuse me Admiral Richmond, Lady Mary." He turned to Jonathan, "I must take the carriage but perhaps the admiral might be prevailed upon to provide you with a mount back to the parsonage?"

"If that wouldn't inconvenience you, sir?" Jonathan said to the admiral. "After time at sea, I need to renew my equestrian skills." And seeing Lady Mary rise to bid farewell to the parson, he rose too.

"Please convey our wishes to the Bagshot family and tell them we shall pray for their father," Lady Mary said.

The parson retreated bowing to all present individually, "Most kind, Lady Mary, most considerate." Middleton escorted him out.

* * * *

"What a relief to be outdoors," Catherine said as Martha closed the parsonage gate behind them. "I'll walk through the village to get my bearings then I'll decide what I want to sketch. Now did you learn those letters I gave you yesterday?"

"Yes, miss, shall I recite the alphabet to you?"

Catherine listened as she began. It pleased her that the maid only stumbled on a few of the letters. "You have done well. I have a slate and scriber with my sketch books. I will show you the shape of a few letters and you can practise them whilst I sketch. I think you might learn to write your name before the end of the day."

"Thank you miss, I have always wanted to be able to sign my name. My mother will be so proud of me when I return home."

They walked on along the high street lined with neat houses. At the village green, the road forked, one way led to the turnpike road, and thus to London, the other to the estates of Penley Court and Witton Abbey. The Blue Bell Inn stood on the edge of the green and served as the coaching house. On the other side of the green, beyond the horse chestnut trees, stood the church.

Catherine stopped, looked both ways before choosing the road past the Smithy and the inn.

She heard the church bell strike the hour and a closed carriage slowed as it turned into the inn yard. Catherine glanced at the driver, quickly at first then observed him more closely. Something about his appearance held her artistic eye. Somehow he looked different from coachmen she had seen before. His thick top coat was layered with several capes, he wore an old style tri-corner hat, and he carried a long musket across his back. There was a fallen tree lying on the edge of the green, the branches had been felled but the trunk remained. She made her way towards it. "Let's take up position here," she said to Martha, who opened the large canvas bag she carried and handed the artist's materials to her mistress.

Catherine had no intention of drawing the coachman, or the gentleman who stepped out. But before long, she had a sketch developing of the rear of the carriage, the gentleman descending, and the driver holding the carriage door open.

Next she drew the letters M-a-r-t-h-a C-o-p-e across the top of the maid's slate. "Now copy each of these in turn, begin with the first large letter M and make the letters curve at the ends."

Martha started with her initial letter and slowly drew across the slate. Catherine watched her closely and couldn't resist doing a quick sketch of the girl and her slate.

The post horn sounded and she looked down the road. The loud pounding of horses' hooves, rattle of coach wheels, and the shout of the coachman drew her away from her work. The Portsmouth Mail coach thundered into the village. Fresh horses were run out of the yard, harnesses unhitched, and hitched. Steamy vapour rose from the backs of the four spent horses as they were led away and mail bags loaded. The coachman bellowed something at the ostler, but Catherine couldn't hear him clearly. She was watching the guard sitting next to the driver on the box. The polished barrel of the blunderbuss he carried glistened in the mid-day sun.

Working swiftly, she drew the outline of the shape they made sitting together. Within minutes, the fresh horses were whipped up and the mail coach took off, London bound.

As the mail coach disappeared round a bend in the road, Catherine returned to her sketch of the inn. She drew the building with its small casement windows and tall stack chimneys. She was adding the final touches to her sketch when the gentleman who had arrived in the closed carriage stepped into the street. She guessed his age to be around thirty as he placed a grey hat on his head. Of portly appearance, his coat was an elegant cut, his breeches light and he wore a pair of highly polished hessians. However, it wasn't his dress that caught her attention but his manner. He had an arrogant stance as he turned to look both ways along the high street. His neck seemed rigid and his nose set permanently at a tilt in the air. As he turned towards her, his puffy cheeks almost poured over the highest pointed collar she had ever seen. How did he manage to turn his head? Was she too fast with her censure? Perhaps the man had suffered some injury and was wearing a neck brace.

He was too interesting a figure not to sketch. Taking up her pencil, she drew a caricature of him in the manner of Mr. Gilray.

* * * *

When Middleton closed the door behind Mr. Winters, Jonathan couldn't hold back any longer. "Sir, what do you know about the death of my father?"

The admiral took in a deep breath, his high forehead creasing. Lady Mary sat down and the admiral signalled for Jonathan to take a chair. "I had the news from Captain Quentin, who in turn got it from his old lieutenant, Mr. Thwaite, who was there. Sir Humphrey had been gambling. He was involved in a card game with my nephew and others. He wagered Aston Grange and lost. Apparently, Granville gave him the opportunity to win it back, which Sir Humphrey accepted. But before play, a note came for Sir Humphrey from his agent and he stepped outside to speak to him. Thwaite stayed inside, heard a shot and rushed outside. Sir Humphrey was lying in the street with a fatal head wound and a pistol at his side."

Jonathan swallowed deeply he had seen men dead and dying before during his life in the service but experience did not ease the pain he felt gripping his insides. He let his head fall forward. It was several moments before he was able to speak, "An unfortunate but swift end."

"Aye lad," the admiral said, "but too many unanswered questions. Quentin said there had been an investigation, but I know no further details. You will have to ask him."

Jonathan looked up expectantly. "Sir, you knew my father—"

"Only slightly, he came to Aston for the summer of my first year here."

"Do you believe him capable of suicide?"

Admiral Richmond shook his head. "I do not know. What goes through a man's mind when he believes he is facing ruin? And what about his other estate? Surely he was still solvent?"

Pain followed by mixed feelings of anger and shame squeezed Jonathan's internal organs. "I discovered yesterday from Bayley at the bank that Westwood House is mortgaged. My father had been gambling heavily since the loss of my mother and brother. I do not know the exact extent of his debts, however, I anticipate a substantive amount but cannot ascertain the level until I speak with his agent in London."

"When do you plan to go to town?" Lady Mary asked.

"Tomorrow, if I can get on the mail coach."

Lady Mary looked at her husband, then back at Jonathan. "Captain and Mrs. Quentin are due back from the Midlands tomorrow. Why not await their return? Quentin might have additional information, or at the very least he can provide you with contacts in town. I believe Mr. Thwaite and his new wife remain there."

The admiral had been sitting in silence, a profound expression on his face. "Do not underestimate my nephew. I have warned him off my property, indeed. I have several grievances against him. He is cunning and leaves little evidence in his wake. How his character became so corrupt, I don't know. My brother was a very successful man in sea-trade he owned a fleet of merchantmen and extensive warehouses. When he died, Granville inherited. But he squandered the money. He refused to take control of his father's business and sold it off to finance his indolent life. When his funds were exhausted, he blamed others, the war, the decline in trade, even pirates. I settled his debts on several occasions until I realised there would be no end to his sloth. I blame his mother. She indulged the boy's every whim. Like my Bella, he was an only child, but his character could not be more different from hers. You may be taken in by him, think him a fool. The man is a charlatan. Do not trust him. He hides his true character behind his foppish manners and dandy apparel. He is pompous, dangerous, and sadistically cruel."

Jonathan had been listening intently, building up a mental picture of the man. "Were there any witnesses, surely the streets of St. James' were teeming with people late at night?"

The admiral nodded, "Aye lad, you would have thought so, but apparently not."

"Mr. Thwaite, your informant, he was there but didn't see my father shoot himself?" Jonathan asked, the more he heard of the incident the more anxious he became to know all the facts.

The admiral leaned forward in his armchair. "Thwaite witnessed the card game like several others present in the club. It was a high stakes match, attracting many to the table. Granville was cunning, he gathered witnesses around him to support his claim. Thwaite stood close, determined to scrutinise the play. He had purpose in his observation."

"Purpose? What do you mean?" Jonathan asked.

"Thwaite had seen Granville play cards before and believed he cheated, but he couldn't prove it. Your father was losing heavily. Thwaite smelt a rat and wanted to expose him, but he lacked proof."

"You need to speak with Quentin," Lady Mary said, "I know he has more he can tell you about Mr. Richmond's movements. I am expecting the Quentins to call tomorrow on their way back to the Grange. Why not join us?"

"I had planned to journey to London tomorrow. I do not feel I could impose upon the parson's hospitality any longer. He has been kindness itself to me and I know he has his own concerns."

"Aye, this auction business for his living, at least I can try to make some recompense there," the admiral said.

"I fear his situation might be more urgent. The notice to quit is for Michaelmas but the Aston parish funds have been withdrawn from the bank on the direction of lawyers acting on behalf of the owner."

"God's Teeth!" the admiral cried. "Is there no end to the man's infamy?"

Lady Mary placed her hand on the admiral's arm. "We must see that the parson does not suffer, it would be embarrassing for him to have creditors queuing at his door when he is preaching the contrary from his pulpit."

The admiral nodded. "Once again, Mary your advice is wise. I shall have a quiet word with him."

"Sir Jonathan," Lady Mary said, "Would you consider dining with us this evening? You could stay overnight and meet the Quentins when they arrive."

"Splendid idea. I don't know why I didn't think of it myself. Always glad of male company at the table." He looked quickly at his wife. "Not that I don't enjoy your company, my dear, but a little news of the action in the Caribbean would not come amiss."

"We dine at five," Lady Mary said.

"Then I shall be only too pleased to accept."

* * * *

Riding proved more exhilarating than Jonathan imagined. It had been over a year since he had been astride a horse and that had been in the heat of the Caribbean. Instead of following the carriage road, he cut across the estate and made for the boundary of Witton Abbey and Aston Grange. He drew rein to take in the view of the river valley. Happy memories of childhood, riding with his father and brother, touched his heart. He took a deep breath and smiled as he caught the hint of the sea on the breeze.

Along the valley, thin trails of smoke rose from the tall chimneys of Aston Grange. Most likely the staff were making the place ready to welcome back their master and mistress. The thought made him slightly envious and he shook his head, as if trying to dismiss it. But the yearning remained. How much he wanted to be the one coming home to a wife and possibly the prospect of family. He had never felt that way before, accepting his postings with joy in his heart and eager anticipation of adventure. Today was different. England was no longer at war in Europe, although there was still action to be had in the Caribbean and north Americas. England had his service for over twenty years, now he wanted England. He craved for the special part of England which stretched out before him—the green acres of his family estate now denied him.

How ironical, only when love is lost does its true importance manifest. He had loved his home and his family. He had vowed to restore the former, but what could he do about the latter? Smiling, he turned his horse and kicked the animal to a trot. Perhaps in time he would have kinfolk of his own again.

As he neared the village, he slowed his mount to a walk and saw a young lady walking ahead with her maid. "Miss Ellis," he called.

She turned and dropped him a brief curtsey. "Good afternoon, Sir Jonathan."

He doffed his hat and smiled down at her as he dismounted. "What a pleasant surprise to find you about the village on this fine day."

"I needed to take the air. Although my aunt was reluctant to part with me, I managed to persuade her that some exercise would be most beneficial. I thought she might have accompanied me, however, she wouldn't leave the parsonage until my uncle returned. Have you seen him on the road? I thought you accompanied him to Witton Abbey?"

"I did indeed, Miss Ellis, but he was called to a sick-bed on the other side of Aston Hill."

"Oh, is that far," she looked about her, "pray in which direction?"

Jonathan smiled again at her as he pointed towards the hills beyond the church on the edge of the village. She had exquisite eyes, large, warm, and brown. Her expression engaging and her manner calm. "I was returning to the parsonage, if you are going in that direction, I would be pleased to escort you."

"Thank you Sir Jonathan, you must have read my mind for I have finished my sketching and Martha has completed her lessons. We were on our way back to the parsonage when you came upon us. Your company would be most welcome."

As they strolled towards the village, two young boys were coming in the opposite direction.

"You lads, I'm Sir Jonathan Westwood. Take this horse to the parsonage. Tell Mr. Winters' stable hand the horse belongs to Admiral Richmond and I shall be along presently." Jonathan flipped a coin at the older boy.

"Yes sir, at once sir," the boy replied.

He watched the lads lead the horse away and then turned to Miss Ellis. "Have you been sketching anything in particular?"

"Only a few buildings and the occasional figure of interest, I might use them in a larger work or painting in the future." She smiled at him and Jonathan felt drawn to her.

"I would like to see your work," he said, "if you would oblige me." His eyes fixed upon her and after a few moments he was unable to tear his gaze away. She broke the eye contact.

"This is the first opportunity I have had to look around the neighbourhood on my own and to stop to draw. Unfortunately, my aunt feels the need to occupy my time, no doubt fulfilling her duties as a good hostess, but I am not the sort of person who demands the company of others perhaps as much as she would like. I am happy to amuse myself drawing or reading."

"Perhaps that makes you a better guest than I, for in truth Miss Ellis, I find the amount of unnecessary talk at the parsonage quite substantive and after only a few hours, quite annoying. It is perhaps fortunate that the need to converse at length is a trait shared by both the Winters."

Her large eyes looked up and caught his, her eyebrows lifted briefly, followed by a slight hum. "I am learning to cope with my aunt's conversation by reciting Mr. Shakespeare's sonnets in my head, but please do not let her know, I would not wish to offend her."

It pleased Jonathan that his remark amused her because he was wondering if he'd been impolite about his host and was about to apologise, but this time it was Jonathan's turn to laugh. "Miss Ellis, at sea with only male company, perhaps we are too blunt. I am ill-practised in the art of delicate conversation but I will try your ploy, although I think the bard's sonnets would be too taxing for me to recall from memory."

"Now Sir Jonathan, perhaps you are not a man of literature but I am sure you have had to learn by heart the Admiralty manual needed for your lieutenant's examination, could you not run through a few paragraphs when my aunt is in full flow?"

"Miss Ellis, that would be most irregular, but I shall certainly try."

They had passed the church and were approaching the village green when a closed carriage trundled out of the inn yard and onto the high street. The driver cracked the whip and the four horses pounded towards them at gathering speed. "Take care, Miss Ellis!" Jonathan shouted, as he put out a protective arm in front of her and pushed her and her maid into a doorway. The driver whipped the team until he had them almost at a gallop and the carriage thundered by, blinds drawn.

"By all the saints," Jonathan cried, "does that man pay no heed to the welfare of his cattle or the lives of innocent bystanders? Are you hurt, Miss Ellis and your maid?" He stepped back to allow them to emerge from their shelter.

"Martha are you hurt?" she asked.

"No, miss, a bit shaken, though. I don't like being nearly run over."

"I think you exaggerate," Catherine said, "I don't think we were in danger. Perhaps the driver didn't expect to see three people walking along."

"Whether he expected us or not, he had no consideration for our well-being when he drove his team out. Please reassure me, Miss Ellis, are you unharmed?" A flicker of concern flashed in her dark eyes and he assumed she was being very brave but didn't want to make a fuss.

"I am fine, Sir Jonathan, thanks to you, but please, let us not say anything of this to my aunt and uncle, or I fear we shall not hear the last of it."

* * * *

Catherine barely had time to sit down after Sir Jonathan left. On discovering that her husband had not returned since leaving for Witton Abbey, Mrs. Winters went into a minor panic. Her behaviour oscillated from nervous concern about the duration of her husband's absence to speculative worry claiming some accident might have befallen him as he had to venture across unmade roads.

Catherine calmed her down with several cups of tea only to find the conversation returned to her future.

"My dear, I could not have been more delighted when I saw you coming back to the parsonage accompanied by Sir Jonathan this afternoon. News will spread, of course, and perhaps it will not be out of the way to have your name linked with his, for he is quite eligible, and there is the title."

"Sir Jonathan has far greater worries than any possible gossip linking my name with his. Besides aunt, I have no desire to enter upon matrimony at present."

"No desire?" Mrs. Winters let out a loud huff and put her cup and saucer down on the table with a rattle. "You are nearly one-and-twenty, very many girls are married by the time they are your age. What can your mother have been thinking all this time? You are a very attractive young lady, an only child, and your father has considerable commercial interests in the north. Were there no young gentlemen in Lancashire who took your interest?"

Catherine bit her lip, perhaps if she told her aunt about Rossi, it might silence her. *No, my Aunt Winters would not rest until she knew all the facts, then she would dwell upon each one until she had feasted on the whole painful affair. Keep your own counsel.* She shook her head.

"No?" Mrs. Winters snapped. "Then that is why we must act swiftly and take advantage of every opportunity. I am bitterly disappointed that Sir Jonathan has removed to Witton. However comfortable Admiral Richmond might make him, I doubt if he will find himself in such congenial company as our family dinner last night. When he sang *Heart of Oak,* my heart swelled with national pride. His voice so clear, and to see the two of you together, I felt certain there was a spark there. And now he has gone from us. However, with Captain and Mrs. Quentin due back tomorrow and still celebrating their nuptials, perhaps a ball at Aston Grange might not be too much to hope for. I shall suggest it to Mrs. Quentin when we next take tea. Catherine, my dear, I can't wait to introduce you to her, she is, after all an exceedingly good friend of mine."

There was the sound of a carriage outside and Mrs. Winters hurried to the window. "It is Mr. Winters returned." She glanced quickly around the room, fluffed up a couple of cushions and went into the hall to welcome her husband.

Catherine took her chance and slipped out through the long open window into the garden. Quietly she made her way around to the kitchen and entered. Cook and a maidservant dropped her short bobs as she crossed the stone floor. Catherine replied by placing her index finger to her lips and disappeared up the back stairs to her room.

Once inside, she flopped onto her bed, lay on her back, hands behind her head, and gazed up at the ceiling. She had enjoyed the day, not only had she escaped the parsonage and her aunt for a few hours, but also she spent time with Sir Jonathan. She liked his smile, the way he looked at her, and his gallant manner when he had leapt to protect her from the carriage. He had stepped close to her, so close she could smell the fragrance of sandalwood on his shaven jaw. She closed her eyes and mentally painted a portrait of him in the finest detail. The wavy hair, tied back in a queue. "I suppose he'll have a haircut when he gets to town," she said, thinking aloud, "but I could make a sketch of him and see how he might appear."

The idea intrigued her. She sat up, swung her legs down from the bed, and retrieved her sketchbook from the canvas bag draped on the chair. Quickly, she flipped over the pages, stopping only briefly at each of the drawings she had done of him. The three-quarter profile, always a favourite pose of hers, caught him at his best. She used the sketch as a reference and began outlining his features. When she came to draw in his hair, deliberately she made his waves shorter until she was satisfied with the finish. Happy with the final drawing, she took out fresh paper and coloured pastels and began working on a larger drawing. "Long hair or the short, Sir Jonathan?" she asked the portrait and waited for a few moments. "Short suits you best," she said to the picture and began working on a fashionable short hairstyle for the drawing.

Some while later, Martha entered to remind her it was time dress for dinner. Catherine looked down at the dress she was wearing, the one she had worn during her afternoon sketching excursion. The hem was muddied and the cuffs dirty from the drawing materials. "I'd better change. Will you be able to clean this gown?"

Martha bent down to examine the dirt marks in closer detail. She rubbed some of the dried mud off with her fingers. "I will soak this gown tomorrow, miss," and began unpinning the bodice and loosening the ties at the neck.

"I'll wear the cream muslin with the green velvet trim," Catherine said.

Martha went to the cupboard and drew a gown out from the carefully laid stack and draped it over her arm. As she crossed the room, she stopped at the new pastel sketch on the table. "Wasn't Sir Jonathan gallant this afternoon? This picture you've done of him, it is wonderful, miss. You've made him look so handsome."

Catherine thought for a few moments. "I've a pencil sketch in my bag I did earlier. Would you like to have it?"

"Oh, miss, you're so generous and good to me. I've been practising my letters."

"Good, now pick up a pencil and write your name on a sheet of paper."

Martha held the pencil awkwardly, making it harder for her to keep her writing even. When she had finished, she held up the piece of paper, a proud smile on her face.

"Very good, you are making excellent progress. Now, I'm going to draw a line with my ruler, when it is done, write your name again along the line. It will help you keep the lettering straight."

Martha did as she was told and showed the result to Catherine.

"Well done Martha," Catherine said. "Today you have learnt to write your own name."

"I'm so grateful to you, miss, for allowing me to learn and teaching me."

"This is only the beginning Martha, I'll not only have you writing soon but also reading books."

Chapter Four

Jonathan placed the quill down on the writing slope and sanded his letter to his agent in London. His brief communication contained details of his expected arrival and the address of his club where he might be contacted. He looked up at the sound of a carriage outside. From his bedroom window he saw a carriage stop at the main entrance to Witton Abbey.

A commanding figure emerged whom he assumed to be Captain Quentin, although he wore plain attire. Dark hair, broad shoulders, and in his mid-thirties, the gentleman held out his hand to the lady, who also descended. Jonathan assumed she was Mrs. Quentin, Admiral Richmond's daughter. She wore a dark coloured spencer and matching bonnet with a white muslin dress. As soon as she had her feet on the ground, she looked up at the Abbey, a broad smile on her face. Jonathan stepped back from the window, he did not want to be caught spying on the newly married couple.

As he did not wish to disturb the welcome between father and daughter, he decided to keep to his room until the admiral requested his presence. It gave him time to reflect how much he had enjoyed the Richmonds' company the previous evening. The dinner had been plain but well-cooked and, therefore, greatly to his liking. He shared many of the admiral's tastes and took pleasure in relating his recent experiences of frigate life in the Caribbean. Lady Mary added much to the conversation. Her experience of the sea and the life of those who joined the service was second to none, and he did not hesitate to tell her so.

"Would you take your wife to sea?" she asked him.

The question, so direct, had disarmed him initially. The thought had never occurred to him before. "I am not married," he said, avoiding the question rather than commit to a definite answer. He had listened intently when Lady Mary described her adventures at sea with her first husband, Captain Rufford, with whom Jonathan, too, had sailed. But avoidance of Lady Mary's question didn't stop him dwelling upon it when he was alone.

He hadn't slept well in a fixed bed. For years a swung-out hammock, or box bed moving with the ship, had been his berth. Whenever on land, he had difficulty sleeping. It was common among sailors used to the movement of the sea. Many found they could not settle permanently on land. However, he did not consider he was one of them until the last two nights. His disturbed slumber was filled with anxious dreams of his father in danger of physical attack and a young woman who rescued both father and son. But her face remained obscured, as if covered by a veil. The urge to follow her proved irresistible and he left his father behind. Over land and sea she beckoned him, like the sirens calling sailors to their doom, but still he pursued her, until he caught her arm and pulled her towards him. The hood of her voluminous cloak slipped from her head, her dark curls tumbled into his hands as he embraced her. His body pressed to hers, he kissed her soft skin until he found her small bow shaped mouth. He woke aware he had dreamt of Miss Ellis in his arms.

There were several pressing matters. Whilst crossing the Atlantic from the Caribbean and relieved of the onus of command, he had planned his life. His position had changed, now he was his father's heir. But the disturbed tone of his father's letter announcing the deaths of his mother and elder brother caused him great concern. His father's rambling sentences and indecipherable writing signalled a much changed man. However, nothing prepared him for the news when he landed in Portsmouth that his father had committed suicide.

Mr. Bayley, the banker, had been curt and unsympathetic when he imparted the news. "Sir Humphrey's accounts have been dormant for several years," he had said. "And I hold several bills on behalf of Sir Humphrey's creditors awaiting payment." Jonathan interpreted the remark as a call for him to offer settlement, but without confirmation from his agent in London, he had no notion if his prize money would cover all outstanding liabilities and informed Bayley of this.

"I would advise settlement as soon as possible," the banker replied, "if only to secure your own credit in London and, of course, locally." Thus Jonathan left the bank with a smaller loan than he had hoped to secure to finance his initial weeks ashore. He needed to get to London urgently to see Palmer, his agent.

There was a knock on his door and a footman entered. "Sir Jonathan, Admiral Richmond requests you join him and Captain Quentin in the library."

"Immediately?"

"I believe so, sir."

Jonathan followed the footman downstairs, straightened his cravat as he crossed the hall, and waited for the manservant to open the library doors for him.

"Ah, there you are, Sir Jonathan," the admiral called across the room from his armchair. "Come, let me present my son-in-law, Captain Ross Quentin."

Hand outstretched, Quentin advanced across the room. "Sir Jonathan, I am exceedingly pleased to make your acquaintance."

"I am very glad to meet you," Jonathan said, matching Quentin's firm handshake. The captain smiled and turned to the young woman now at his side. "Sir Jonathan, this is Mrs. Quentin, Admiral Richmond's daughter." Jonathan made the customary bow and she replied with a small curtsey.

"Now all the formalities are over, perhaps we can get down to the important business of Aston Grange," the admiral said from his armchair. "Be seated everyone, I can't talk up to you all."

Mrs. Quentin took a seat next to Lady Mary and near to the admiral. The two men sat opposite each other, forming a half-circle around the admiral, as if expecting him to be the senior voice and lead the discussion.

"Papa, do you wish Mary and me to stay?"

"Yes, my dear I do, for you both know as much about this unfortunate situation as we do. There has to be a resolution and I am open to suggestions from any quarter. Besides, I swear you two often get the best ideas. We mere mortal men simply do as we are ordered. Isn't that so Quentin?"

"Most of the time, sir." The captain chuckled.

The admiral cleared his throat and, looking directly at Jonathan, said, "Sir Humphrey was cheated out of Aston Grange by my nephew. Do not ask me to utter that man's name in my household because I have vowed not to. The mere mention of him makes my blood boil and that, according to my wife, is bad for my constitution. Having stolen the Grange from its rightful owner, I believe my nephew's paid lackeys set upon Sir Humphrey and killed him, thus ensuring he could make no counter claim upon ownership of the estate."

Quentin straightened his back. "We need proof."

"Of course we need proof," the admiral returned sharply. "That is why Sir Jonathan is here, but the crime occurred in London. If witnesses are to be found, they'll be in St. James' where the man fell. You must go to London Sir Jonathan, and I advise you go too, Quentin."

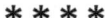

"Are you feeling unwell, Aunt?" Catherine asked as they sat together in the small parlour. Mrs. Winters had hardly spoken a word since breakfast.

"I was thinking...Oh, no. Mr. Winters said my lips must be sealed but I cannot endure the weight of this terrible worry on my shoulders. I have pains surging through my body. I do not think I shall ever sleep again such is the magnitude of the disaster which has befallen us."

Catherine put down the sketch she was working on and joined her aunt on the settee. "Is there anything I can get you to ease your distress?"

"No, nothing." She sniffed and pulled a lace trimmed handkerchief from her sleeve. She dabbed her eyes with it.

"Perhaps you could tell me some of what ails you, it is said that a problem shared is a problem halved."

She tapped her niece's hand. "You are such a good girl, and I have no right to burden you with our difficulties, but I must tell someone. Mr. Winters, himself in a state of high melancholy, imparted the most severe news to me this morning. I can scare believe it, and would not do so, had it not come from his own lips." She gripped Catherine's wrist tightly. "I must have your word that all I say is in confidence but I cannot keep this dreadful news inside me any longer."

"Be assured Aunt Winters, I will be most discreet."

Her aunt sniffed back more tears. "I hope Mr. Winters will forgive me, but he has received notice to quit!"

Catherine thought for a few moments. Should she sympathise or ask for further clarification? It would be crass to pry into her uncle and aunt's affairs, especially if the reason for the notice might cause acute embarrassment. "Do you refer to the parsonage or my uncle's ministry?"

"Both!" She burst into tears. "But worse, we shall be cast out to live, goodness knows where. The living, you see...is in the gift of the Grange...and it's to be sold by auction. Mr. Winters says the admiral and Lord Norton will endeavour to purchase...and that is our only hope, otherwise we must quit by Michaelmas."

"How distressing for you." Catherine put a comforting arm around her aunt's shoulder. "Try not to fret so. I shall say nothing of this to anyone. We must be very discreet and go about the parish business as if nothing is amiss."

Catherine's aunt sniffed several times and nodded. "You have a very wise head on your young shoulders. Your mother must be very proud of you."

Catherine smiled. Her mother had not imparted words of pride when Catherine revealed the plan to elope with Mr. Rossi.

* * * *

The next morning Catherine took her place next to her aunt in church. It was Sunday, and all of Aston's parishioners were expected to attend morning service. The single repetitive clang of the tenor bell echoed from the church tower, a very solemn sound to Catherine's ears. Their box seat was in the front row of the pews, so she couldn't turn around to see the church filling up. Since arriving, Catherine had not heard her uncle deliver a sermon. She waited in nervous anticipation. Of course, neither the butterflies flapping in her stomach, nor her constant need to squeeze her fingers together had anything to do with the imminent arrival of the party from Witton Abbey. But what if Sir Jonathan wasn't with them? What if he had already left for London? Her heart sank—her fidgeting was entirely due to a certain gentleman.

As they rose to sing the first hymn, Catherine stood on tip-toe and scanned the congregation over her shoulder for a hint of his dark wavy hair. His clear tenor voice, reaching the higher notes with tone accuracy made her glance over her other shoulder to where she assumed he was standing. She caught him looking at her. Quickly she tore her eyes away as the warmth of a blush pinked her cheeks.

Mr. Winters sounded very pious as he preached his sermon from the pulpit. However, the brevity of the lesson surprised her. At home, their vicar could easily spend a full hour delivering his weekly message to the parish. They sang a few more hymns and were soon at the church door where Mr. Winters hovered to greet his parishioners.

"Stay close," Mrs. Winters whispered to Catherine, "I must introduce you to Lady Mary and Mrs. Quentin for they will surely invite us to tea within the next few days. As I told your mother, we have the acquaintance of the best families in the neighbourhood."

Dutifully, Catherine stood beside her aunt, pleased that her temper had been restored from the upset of the previous afternoon. Soon, a tall, broad-shouldered gentleman accompanied by a neatly dressed, bright eyed blonde lady emerged with Sir Jonathan. Catherine swallowed deeply, sensing a tell-tale flush colour her cheeks as the newly wedded couple passed a few brief words with Mr. Winters.

"Here is our chance." Aunt Winters nudged her. "I hope Sir Jonathan comes over."

In her heart, Catherine hoped so too, as she experienced an overwhelming feeling of joy when she was near him.

"Good morning, Miss Ellis," Sir Jonathan said. "I doubt if you have been introduced to Captain and Mrs. Quentin. Please allow me to complete the formalities."

Catherine dropped a small curtsey of acknowledgement to him and he proceeded to introduce the newly married couple.

"I understand from Sir Jonathan you draw exceedingly well, Miss Ellis, perhaps you might like to call at the Grange and bring some of your sketches?" Mrs. Quentin said.

Catherine smiled at the young lady and admired her elegant dress and ease of manner. They were of a similar age, although Mrs. Quentin was perhaps a couple of years older.. "I would be very happy to do so, Mrs. Quentin."

"My niece is very talented she draws, sings, and plays. It has been a delight to have her staying at the parsonage. I can't thank her mother enough for sparing her," Mrs. Winters said.

"I think my aunt exaggerates my talents. I do enjoy drawing and painting and would be happy to bring my books and materials to Aston Grange, Mrs. Quentin. With regard to my singing and playing, I prefer not to exhibit my talents outside of my own circle."

"We had the great pleasure of hearing Sir Jonathan sing whilst he was with us," Mrs. Winters said. "He is a noteworthy tenor. Have you heard him perform?"

Mrs. Quentin shook her head. "It appears we have that pleasure to come. Please excuse me, my father is still not well enough to attend Sunday service, however, my stepmother is coming out of church and I must speak with her."

Catherine stood at her aunt's side as Mrs. Quentin approached a tall lady dressed in pale green silk. The manner of their greeting indicated they were more than merely connected, but good friends. Catherine tried to fix a mental picture of them to put into a sketch when she returned to the parsonage. Taller than average, Lady Mary's upright frame was crowned with an abundance of red wiry hair. Taming her tresses must undoubtedly be a taxing job for her maid as a few stray tendrils of hair had escaped the matching silk cap with gold tassel Lady Mary wore. Her face, although plain, had character and her expression appeared most engaging as she spoke to her stepdaughter. She appeared to have an honest disposition—if looks alone could determine character. Catherine glanced quickly at her aunt, then back at the two ladies. Her aunt would be just as anxious to know what the ladies were talking about as she was, so she wasn't surprised to feel a slight nudge at her elbow, and turned back to face her aunt.

"Look, they are coming this way," her aunt said, a broad grin spreading across her round face.

Catherine smiled and hoped she would be introduced to her ladyship. As Sir Jonathan was staying with the Richmonds, an invitation to Witton Abbey might provide her with an opportunity of seeing him again after today. She bit her lip. Every time she saw him a warm sensation filled her, a chance meeting, a stolen glance, a look, or even to be in the same room with him gave her pleasure. There was no denying it; she had developed a *tendre* for him and after only a few meetings over the expanse of a few days. He was so different from Rossi. She shook her head, as if to drive all thought of the Venetian from her head. Could she be falling in love with Sir Jonathan? Quickly she dismissed the notion as Lady Mary and Mrs. Quentin approached.

"Good morning, Mrs. Winters," Lady Mary said.

Aunt Winters dropped a brief curtsey. "Good morning your ladyship, I hope you are well."

"Most certainly, you know I enjoy robust health, but enough of me, I understand you have a guest at the parsonage?" she said smiling at Catherine.

"Lady Mary, please allow me to introduce Miss Ellis, our niece from Lancashire."

She held out her hand to Catherine, who touched her ladyship's fingers and dropped a slight curtsey. "I am very pleased to make your acquaintance Miss Ellis, however, I have the advantage over you as your reputation as an artist has already been made known to me. Sir Jonathan spoke highly of your work and I would be delighted to see some of your sketches, whenever it is convenient for you to call. " She turned to Catherine's aunt, whose mouth was open.

Her cheeks burned with a blush but wasn't quite sure if it was the invitation to Witton Abbey or the knowledge that Sir Jonathan had mentioned her name to the Richmonds.

"As always it would be an honour to call," her aunt said. "I am sure Catherine will be only too pleased to bring her sketch books with her. As for Sir Jonathan, what a gentleman he is, how kind of him, how thoughtful to have mentioned our own dear niece."

Catherine felt obliged to say something before her aunt caused more embarrassment with her praise. "Thank you, Lady Mary. I would be delighted to call and bring my work."

"Perhaps Tuesday or Wednesday would be convenient," Lady Mary said.

* * * *

The Portsmouth-to-London mail coach rattled along the road at a cracking pace, at least eight miles per hour, more if the four horse team were pushed. The coach had priority over any other vehicle on the road—the driver had to reach London before nightfall. The teams of horses were changed regularly as they were spent, but there was no time for passengers to disembark and leisurely stretch their legs. Jonathan huddled to his side of the mail coach and stretched out his long legs, occasionally he glanced across at his two companions, Captain Quentin and his man, Jackson, both squeezed amongst the piles of mailbags. They had been fortunate to secure the seats and as a fourth passenger had not joined them, they were able to plan their strategy during the journey.

"I need to call upon my prize-agent and discover what news he has for me from the Prize Court," Jonathan said.

Captain Quentin nodded his agreement. "In that quest we are as one, although I called upon my man when I was first ashore in the spring, I am hoping he has further news for me. Now I am married, the urgency to purchase an estate grows. There was a time when I considered making Sir Humphrey an offer, indeed, his agent was most encouraging and offered to open negotiations. Now, residing at the Grange has lost its initial appeal for me. It is rightfully yours."

"You are most generous, Captain Quentin," Jonathan said.

"Please call me Ross, we shall be spending most of our time in each other's company over the next few days, I see no need for formality."

"Then please call me Jonathan, I have only been ashore a few days and the title rubs ill with me."

"I suggest we call upon our agents first thing on the morrow. Jackson, you can carry a note to Mr. Thwaite, whom I believe is still at his family's town house."

"Aye, aye, captain," he replied with a salute.

"Jonathan, I suggest we meet at your father's club in St. James' tomorrow evening. Are you still a member?"

"I've no reason to believe White's has blackballed me in my absence."

"I suggest we put up at Fladong's in Oxford Street," Ross said. "The place is well known to old salts. We have a fair chance of finding a few old comrades in arms there. Thwaite appointed an agent for me who investigated Mr. Granville Richmond. He is a cunning fox, known to use several aliases and has a habit of disappearing at will."

"Sounds akin to some of the French frigates we used to chase."

"I chased—Good God! We're under fire!" The coach gathered speed, more shots were fired, and a loud boom came from close by.

"The guard's fired back, sir," Jackson cried as he climbed over the mail bags and lent out of the window.

"Get down man," Ross shouted, "or do you want to get your head blown off?"

Jackson slid back to the floor between the mail bags as the coach swung from side to side.

"He's trying to outrun them," Jonathan shouted, "damned highwaymen. If I were at sea I'd soon give them what for!"

"You and me both," Ross shouted back as they were tossed around by the violent movement of the carriage. "Hold on." As the pace of the coach slowed, Jackson stuck his head out of the window again. "Are you determined to get your brains blow out man?"

"They're taking flight, three of them." Jackson returned to his seat on top of several mail bags.

"Are highwaymen a problem?" Jonathan asked.

Ross drew his hand through his dark hair, "I've been back in England a few months but for some poor souls, times are desperate. Thousands of sailors are ashore, knowing nothing else but the sea. We train them to fight, dangle the prospect of ship prize money in front of them if they'll take the risk and board an enemy vessel. You and I know our cannon could blast the enemy out of the water if we had a mind to. But that wouldn't make our fortunes or provide for our men. I've taken a ship in a few slender hours and each of my men earned more in prize money than he got in a year as a cooper or a caulker's mate. The state of the nation's economy is poor. The war gave rise to trade, ship building, and victualing. But look at the ship's chandlers in Portsmouth. Trade has never been so bad."

"So desperate men risk the noose to make ends meet?"

"Aye, more's the pity."

"And the Peace, will it last?" Jonathan asked.

Ross shrugged and reached for his hat, which he'd lost in the chase, "Who knows, perhaps Boney will do us all a favour and invade."

* * * *

Mrs. Winters was determined to take Catherine to call upon Lady Mary at the earliest opportunity. "Mr. Winters I shall require the carriage after breakfast this morning. Catherine and I have a very important engagement at Witton Abbey today."

"And what if I get another call to attend Bagshot?" he asked, frowning his displeasure.

"You will have to postpone your call or journey back with whichever Bagshot son has summoned you. Catherine and I have been invited and one simply cannot ignore a request from her ladyship. There is always a curricle to be hired from the blacksmithy or inn, should an emergency arise. It is very important to us to maintain my friendship with Lady Mary."

Catherine kept silent throughout the conversation. It was not her place to intervene between husband and wife. However, she had looked forward to calling upon Lady Mary since the Sunday service when the invitation had been extended. Aunt Winters had described the house in great detail and Catherine wanted to see the interior. Sir Jonathan wouldn't be there. According to Mr. Winters, he and Captain Quentin had already left for London, but to walk the same rooms, to glance up at the portraits and paintings, and to see what he had seen, excited her. To be asked to take her sketch book and possibly work whilst her aunt and Lady Mary chatted was an eagerly anticipated prospect not to be missed.

Her aunt did not delay after breakfast was done. She hurried Catherine upstairs to change her gown. "Your best," she insisted in a half-whisper, "you must look your best."

With Martha's help, Catherine dressed in a pale blue velvet spencer and matching bonnet over a white muslin gown with a blue sprig. The colour went well against her dark brown curls, which Martha arranged around the inner brim of her bonnet. When she emerged, lace half-mittens and reticule in hand, her aunt was waiting at the foot of the stairs.

"Come, come, my dear, we haven't a moment to lose."

Although it wasn't a long journey to Witton Abbey, Catherine's aunt kept up an unbroken tirade of words from the whole of Lady Mary's life story to the early spring arrival of the dashing Captain Quentin .

"He was highly sought after," she said, but before Catherine could speak her aunt ran on. "But now we have another in our midst, and a title too. Goodness, what good fortune you came to stay at exactly the same time as Sir Jonathan chose to return to us. I think it is fate, my dear. And to have him speak so highly of you to Lady Mary, well I could hardly contain myself. Oh, what a match it would be."

Catherine had to intervene before her aunt became totally absorbed in matchmaking. "Aunt Winters, you must not carry on so—"

"Carry on, carry on, why ever not? When a titled gentleman speaks in praise of an unattached your lady of quality it can mean only one thing. Be happy my dear, for I am convinced when Sir Jonathan is restored to his estates, he will be at the parsonage down on his knees making you an offer."

The heat of a deep blush swept over Catherine's cheeks. This could not be. She did like him and he did have a profound effect upon her when she was in close proximity to him. There were a few moments when she had questioned whether she might be falling in love with him. But despite what her heart wished, her head spoke wisely. *Fall in love with him as much as you like, he might promise you the world, but can you trust a man again?*

The carriage stopped outside the entrance to Witton Abbey, an imposing frontage greatly modified to the Palladian style from the original Tudor timber framed structure. Catherine stepped out after her aunt and gazed in awe at the house. They were greeted by the butler.

"Lady Mary is expecting us, Middleton. This is Miss Ellis."

Middleton took their parasols and placed them on the hall table. "May I take the bag for you Miss Ellis," he asked.

"No thank you," Catherine replied, "I wish to keep it with me."

He lifted a slight disapproving eyebrow before escorting them to the small parlour. Lady Mary stood up when her butler announced the visitors. But she wasn't alone, Mrs. Quentin was with her. After the formal greetings, Lady Mary invited her guests to sit down. "Refreshments please, Middleton, and as it is warm outside today, perhaps some cordial?" When the butler had closed the door behind him, she continued, "Captain Quentin has gone to London with Sir Jonathan on business, so Bella has come to stay until he returns."

"How considerate of your ladyship," Catherine's aunt nodded, "and how unfortunate to be separated from your husband so soon after your return home, Mrs. Quentin. But do you not feel strange in your former home, now you are no longer mistress of the establishment?"

Catherine bit her lower lip, why did her aunt have an aptitude for saying the wrong things at the most inappropriate moments?

Mrs. Quentin smiled. "For my part, I shall always feel at home at Witton, Mrs. Winters, however, I could not have rescinded my position as its mistress to any one finer than my dear friend."

Catherine noted the ease in Bella Quentin's manner and how unperturbed she appeared by Aunt Winters' remark.

"Now Miss Ellis, how do you find our neighbourhood?" Lady Mary asked.

"I find the scenery very different from my home in the north. Your chalk hills, fields, and deep cut valleys are most attractive. I enjoyed our trip to Portsmouth, if only to see the sea again."

"We spent several hours at the draper's emporium and called into the dressmakers. Catherine wanted to order a couple of new gowns." Mrs. Winters said.

"Do you like the sea, Miss Ellis?"

"Yes, Mrs. Quentin, I do. Instead of coming over land, Papa and I took a packet out of Liverpool and were able to come all the way to Portsmouth. I have never sailed before but found the whole experience very invigorating, although we scarce lost sight of the land except when we crossed the Bristol Channel."

"Both Bella and I are great lovers of the sea, perhaps that is why we chose to marry into the service," Lady Mary said, a broad smile creeping across her freckled face.

"If I had been born a boy, Miss Ellis, I would have been sent to sea and welcomed the opportunity," Mrs. Quentin said, "alas few ladies have the chance of a life on the ocean wave, my stepmother, however, is very much the exception."

Aunt Winters nodded her agreement, "Lady Mary has some wonderful tales of her life sailing with her first husband. Indeed, Catherine, her knowledge of the sea and geography of the world is second to none. Isn't that so, Mrs. Quentin?"

"Indeed, there is no praise sufficient to do justice to my stepmother's knowledge of naval matters, but Miss Ellis, we are neglecting you. I understand you are a talented artist. Lady Mary has it on good authority that we should see some of your work. Have you brought your sketch books with you?"

"Yes," Catherine replied and removed two of her books from the canvas bag she had brought with her. She handed one to Lady Mary and the other to Mrs. Quentin. Both ladies began leafing through the books.

"You are indeed talented, Miss Ellis, why I recognize several of these people from the village," Lady Mary said.

"And here are several likenesses of Sir Jonathan," Mrs. Quentin added.

"I like to draw almost everyone I meet," Catherine confessed. "I enjoy nothing more than going out and sketching not only the places I see, but also people about their daily tasks."

"Oh, Mary, look at this," Mrs. Quentin held out the sketch book to her ladyship and pointed to one of the drawings, her eyes flashed at Catherine. "Where did you see this gentleman and when?" She turned the sketch book around and indicated the caricature of the arrogant gentleman outside the inn.

"He came in a closed carriage on Saturday and went into the inn." Catherine said.

Mrs. Quentin frowned, Lady Mary looked concerned, and Aunt Winters squinted at the book. "What has Catherine been drawing? I can't see as well as I used to, Mr. Winters says I must obtain some spectacles for close work."

"Is there anything the matter?" Catherine asked bewildered that one of her drawings, albeit a mere cartoon done in Mr. Gillray's lampooning style, should provoke close attention.

Lady Mary straightened her back, "That is Mr. Granville Richmond, who believes himself the new owner of Aston Grange. We are not pleased to know he has been in the neighbourhood."

"Oh, dear," Catherine said, "have I offended the gentleman or yourselves by drawing him so? Only it was his stance and high-handed manner that amused me. I could not resist portraying him thus. Please forgive me if I have caused offence to one of your family."

"My dear Catherine, I hope you do not mind me calling you so, you have done nothing wrong," Lady Mary said. "You have captured his likeness, mannerism, and stance exceedingly well, but this is the gentleman Sir Jonathan and Captain Quentin have gone to London to confront regarding the Westwood estates. To receive intelligence that he was on our doorstep only a few days ago is most important."

Mrs. Quentin, who had remained silent throughout her stepmother's explanation, said, "Thank you, Miss Ellis, for being so observant. I shall write to my husband immediately. I'm sure Sir Jonathan will be grateful to hear the news, too."

A warm feeling swelled in Catherine's heart. The knowledge that in some small way, her work was of use to Sir Jonathan gave her infinite satisfaction.

Chapter Five

Early next morning Jonathan and Ross stood outside the Thwaite townhouse in Piccadilly awaiting entry. The door opened and a stern-faced butler bade them entry. No sooner had they stepped across the threshold, than Jonathan saw a plainly dressed gentleman bouncing downstairs towards them.

"Dashed glad to see you, Ross, as ever you are most welcome."

"Sir Jonathan, let me introduce Mr. Jeremy Thwaite, my former second-in-command and long time friend."

"Sir, you don't know how pleased I am to make your acquaintance. I only wish our meeting was under more favourable circumstances." Mr. Thwaite held out his hand.

Jonathan took it and immediately felt the bond of another officer. Thwaite wasn't as tall as the captain he had served. His neat light brown hair was clipped in the latest fashion. His face was broad, his eyes large, and his nose well-shaped, obviously he had been handy with his fists as a young mid-shipman as no other middy had managed to rearrange the shape of his nose. His large head gave him an unusual top-heavy appearance as the rest of his body was quite lean. "The pleasure is mine and please, we are no longer at sea, call me Jonathan."

The younger man's eyes lit up. "Only if you'll call me Jeremy."

"Come along, gentlemen, we have no time to lose on the niceties of first name terms. We have work to do."

"Indeed, perhaps we can talk in my study." Jeremy pointed in the direction of a door at the far end of the hall and led the way. He turned briefly to the butler. "We do not want to be disturbed by anyone, do you understand?"

"Yes, sir, does that include Mrs. Thwaite?" The butler asked.

Jeremy paused for a moment, looked at Ross and then at Jonathan, as if silently seeking some sort of signal. When none was given, he replied, "Yes." The butler left closing the door behind him.

"Now, gentlemen," Jeremy said, "where do we begin?"

"We need details," Ross replied. "You were one of the last people to see Sir Humphrey alive. I know you have been through this before, but perhaps there is a small detail which has been overlooked?"

"I recall seeing Sir Humphrey gambling at White's; he was heavily into the tables when I arrived. There was a buzz around the place, you know the sort of thing. Naturally, I was surprised to see him. He had been an acquaintance of my father's some while ago, but I hardly recognised him. His complexion had turned very ruddy and he had developed a stoop, in short, he had aged considerably."

"I know from his letter bearing the tragic news of my mother and brother that he had taken their loss very much to heart," Jonathan said. "His words rambled and his writing had become a scrawl. I became worried about him and decided to return home."

"On the first occasion I saw him gambling, he wrote several promissory notes to keep himself in the game. I didn't know it at the time, but one of the players was Granville Richmond."

"Where do I find this gentleman?" Jonathan said, his anger rising, "I've a mind to call him out."

"Steady on," Ross said, "you are not the only one who would like revenge on Richmond, but first you'd never get him on the other end of a duelling pistol and live to tell the tale. Second, he is as elusive as a fox when he has a mind to go to ground, and third, he has his fingers in several cesspits. Gambling is only a pastime to him—I believe he is behind a white slavery gang and smuggling. These are hanging offences, but without witnesses prepared to swear evidence against him in a court of law, he is free to roam at will."

"You both believe he was responsible for my father's death?"

"Aye." Ross and Jeremy replied in unison.

Jonathan locked at Jeremy. "Tell me more about my father's gambling."

"As I explained, that was the first occasion. Someone must have said something in the club, perhaps a sleight of hand was seen between

Richmond and his cohort. A footman riveted one of the players' hands to the table and the game was declared null and void. All monies were returned to the players. Richmond wasn't directly involved, otherwise he would have been banned from the club and his name struck from the membership. But he got away with it. He was anchoring after the Grange then, suggesting, ever so politely that Sir Humphrey should back up his notes with collateral."

"Why did Richmond want the Grange?" Jonathan asked.

Ross let out a long sigh. "That's the very question I raised with the admiral. As the admiral's nearest male relation, Granville believes he is the admiral's rightful heir. He wanted to marry Bella to secure his inheritance, but she refused him. Thus rejected, he sought revenge. We think he is in league with the gang of French pirates who abducted Bella."

"Abduction? Admiral Richmond's daughter was abducted?"

Ross nodded. "Before Bella and I were married. If it hadn't been for Jeremy and my crew's diligence manning the admiral's sloop we would never have caught up with them."

"But Richmond? Did he escape?"

"He wasn't foolish enough to sail with them, no he had other plans for Bella once she landed in France," Ross said.

"We must find proof," Jeremy pleaded. "Richmond has disgraced his family, betrayed his kin, and cheated you out of your rightful inheritance,

Jonathan. We must act swiftly and bring an end to this man's evil reign."

Jonathan dragged his hand through his long wavy hair, still styled with a queue in the manner of a naval officer. His head hung low, the task before them seemed insurmountable. "How?"

"Jeremy, give us the details again of the night Sir Humphrey was killed," Ross said, "there might be some small clue we have missed."

"Of course," Jeremy nodded. "The night he died, he was involved in a game at White's, as before. Richmond took his promissory notes up to a point then asked him to back them with one of his estates. I do not know if he offered Westwood House, initially, but I suspect Richmond was only interested in the Grange. He wanted it because of its proximity to the admiral's land and, possibly, a good location near to Portsmouth for his other clandestine activities."

"What happened between the end of the wager and my father leaving the club?"

"That's the strange part. Richmond made a grand gesture, offered to wager all your father had lost on one turn of the cards. Your father accepted—he had nothing more to lose and everything to gain. But before the wager was transacted, he received a note, said it was urgent with his agent and he would be back shortly. You can imagine the excitement in the club, dozens of members gathered around to witness the final turn of the cards. We heard a shot. I rushed outside with several others. Sir Humphrey's body lay in the road, the street deserted, a pistol in his hand."

Jonathan swallowed deeply, although he was coming to terms with his father's death, to have the scene drawn so vividly caused him heartache.

"Jeremy, when you saw the body, how was Sir Humphrey lying? Can you recall?" Ross asked.

"On his back with his pistol at his fingertips."

"Show us, lie on the floor in the same manner," Ross said, "and take this statuette, it's about the same weight as a pistol."

Jeremy jumped up, took the figure and went to the centre of the room where he lay on the floor.

"Are you sure Sir Humphrey was found like that?" Ross asked.

"Aye, it was a shock but I remember it as if it were yesterday."

"Jonathan, which hand did your father use to shoot with?"

A cold stab like a dagger pierced Jonathan's heart. "My father used his right hand to write, he had been whipped as a boy by his governess until he mastered the quill and his letters, but in all other tasks he favoured the left and had his guns specially adapted when necessary."

Ross jumped to his feet. "As we suspected. Sir Humphrey was murdered."

"But Ross, where is the proof?" Jeremy asked.

Ross put his hand to his dimpled chin. "I don't know, gentlemen, but we must find it."

* * * *

"Was that a carriage I heard pull up outside?" Catherine's aunt asked her as they sat in the small parlour after breakfast. Mr. Winters had retreated to his study at the back of the parsonage.

Catherine went to the window. "Indeed it is, aunt, and Lady Mary and Mrs. Quentin are descending."

"Quick! Fluff up the cushions, hide the sewing, and help me off with this apron."

Hurriedly Catherine did as her aunt bid, rolling the apron up and tucking it into her aunt's sewing box. They were stood waiting calmly when the parlour maid opened the door and announced the guests.

"What a wonderful surprise," Catherine's aunt enthused and dropped a brief curtsy to the ladies. "Catherine and I had no notion when we parted yesterday, we would have the pleasure of seeing you both so soon. Please, come, sit down, we were discussing which charity calls we would undertake today. If the weather remains fair, we could venture as far as Abbeyfields farm. Mrs. Martin has recently been confined and given birth to a daughter. I was only saying to Catherine she might not have the joy of seeing so young a baby until she has her own, should she be so blessed."

Catherine blinked. Her aunt had said nothing of the sort. The new Martin baby was news to her. She pressed her lips together and hoped her initial look of surprise wasn't noticed by the guests.

Lady Mary settled in an armchair and Mrs. Quentin sat on the settee next to Catherine.

"Would you like some refreshment?" Catherine's aunt asked, but without waiting for an answer, rang her bell. The parlour maid must have been waiting outside the door because she entered the room immediately.

"Hot chocolate, biscuits, and cakes," her aunt ordered. The maid dropped a curtsey, acknowledged her mistress' order, and went to prepare the tray.

"We have a slight problem, Mrs. Winters," Lady Mary said once the maid had left the room, "and we were hoping that you and Miss Ellis might be able to help us."

Aunt Winters was all smiles. "Oh, most certainly, be assured, Lady Mary, Catherine and I would wish to help you in whatever capacity we can."

Lady Mary grinned back at her. "As you know Captain Quentin has gone to London on business with Sir Jonathan and Bella has been staying at Witton with us, but she is anxious to return to her own establishment, having spent so little time there."

"In truth, Mrs. Winters," Mrs. Quentin said, "I was wondering if you could spare Miss Ellis for a few days whilst the captain is away. I would so much like some company at the Grange for I only have my maid, Miss Roberts."

"Oh, what a generous offer, Catherine, you must accept. Of course, I shall miss your delightful company but I feel Mrs. Quentin's need is by far the greater." A broad smile divided her round face.

Catherine's heart leapt. The invitation was a blessing. Although she didn't dislike staying at the parsonage, her room was comfortable and her aunt kept a good table, however, the persistent dialogue, usually nothing more than utter trivia, had become irksome. A few days break in fresh surroundings with female company nearer her own age was the answer to her prayers. "Lady Mary, Mrs. Quentin, I would be delighted to stay at Aston Grange for a few days."

Lady Mary clapped her hands together. "We are agreed then. Of course, you understand, I would have been only too happy to stay with Bella, but until the admiral's leg is fully healed my duty, as a wife, is at his side."

The way Lady Mary smiled gave Catherine the impression she was trying to flatter her aunt..

"A wife must always put her husband first, mustn't she, Catherine?" Aunt Winters said, smiling as if she had just imparted great words of wisdom.

Catherine nodded her agreement but kept silent.

"My reasons for wanting female company are very selfish," Mrs. Quentin confessed. "Whilst it was most commendable of my husband to employ his former crew as household staff, it does create a certain measure of awkwardness. No doubt, in time the matter will be resolved when I can engage some housemaids and other female servants. Indeed, I did think of using some of the staff from Penley. But Lady Mary heard only this morning that Lord and

Lady Norton will be arriving soon with their household to spend the remainder of the summer there. Thus the Penley staff will be fully engaged."

"How wonderful for the neighbourhood and, of course, for your ladyship, to have your family close by," Catherine's aunt said.

A knock on the door brought two housemaids, now wearing fresh aprons, into the parlour carrying two large trays of biscuits, small sandwiches, and cakes. Two pots of steaming chocolate filled the room with a pleasant aroma.

Catherine felt a light touch of Mrs. Quentin's hand on her sleeve. "Do you have a maid to accompany you?"

"Yes, I have girl I am training, Miss Cope."

"Good," Mrs. Quentin replied, "my maid, Miss Roberts, will be pleased to instruct her. She has done nothing but moan since we returned from honeymoon about the excessive number of menservants in the captain's household. She refuses to take her meals in the servants' hall and dines alone off a tray. I believe she will welcome your Miss Cope."

"When would you like us to come?" Catherine asked.

"I shall return to the Grange tomorrow, perhaps I can call by at noon and collect you? And Miss Ellis, will you please bring your art materials with you? I have to confess I have an ulterior motive, would you consider painting my portrait?"

Catherine's heart leapt. Mrs. Quentin was offering her a commission. "I have colour pastels with me and watercolours, but if you wish me to work in oils, I shall have to send home for supplies and canvas."

"Please allow me to acquire them, I'm sure we can arrange for the materials, if you will draw up a list, perhaps Captain Quentin can purchase them in London and either bring them back with him or arrange transportation."

"Mrs. Quentin, I am breathless," Catherine panted. "It would give me great pleasure to accept your most generous offer. However, there is no need to trouble your husband, I have a large supply of art materials at home and can send for them."

* * * *

Jonathan stood outside the formidable building housing a number of prize agents' offices. His man, Palmer, had been housed there for several years, or at least he hoped he was still there. As he looked up and down the street, apprehension gripped his stomach. He had entered the bank in Portsmouth with confidence, a gentleman of substance, only to find the Westwood accounts empty and his father dead. He took a deep breath, silently praying all would be well, that his prize money would be sufficient perhaps to settle his father's account and buy the mortgage on Westwood House. As for Aston Grange, he put the estate to the back of his mind as far as he could.

Every time he thought of the place his hackles rose. He wanted revenge and would take it when he came face-to-face with Granville Richmond.

He was pleased to find Mr. Palmer's name listed on the brass plate outside of the building and went inside.

A red-cheeked man greeted him and invited him into his small office. Palmer wore a wig of the old style, a long coat, grey breeches, and a pair of wire-rimmed spectacles balanced on the end of his large nose. "Sir Jonathan, I thought I might find you crossing my threshold. My condolences regarding your father." He shook his hand.

"Thank you, I am here on business, Mr. Palmer," Jonathan said determined to keep their conversation short. "What monies do you have for me in my prize account?"

"Please take a seat." He waited for his client to sit before resuming his own seat behind his desk. He signalled to his clerk, "Bring me Captain Westwood's ledger."

A few moments later, a young man emerged from behind the racks of ledgers and books carrying a volume which he placed on Mr. Palmer's desk. The young man retreated, closing the door behind him.

Mr. Palmer opened the ledger and turned over several pages until he found the last entry, running his finger down the column he looked up at Jonathan. "Your account stands at ten thousand, six hundred and twenty-three pounds, fourteen shillings, and three pence. A tidy sum, sir, but that doesn't include the

prize money for the French frigate *Argent* captured in
'99. Alas, the Prize Court is still sitting on that bounty
sir, despite re-commissioning the vessel. Now we
have so many laid up, their value has been halved, if
they can be sold. Some have been demasted and put
to prison hulks, a pitiful sight, if I might say, sir. Many
are anchored down the estuary alongside the
marshlands—at least your bounty isn't amongst
them."

Jonathan scratched his head, for a gentleman
returning from sea, his prize money would have been
sufficient to secure him a comfortable life, but with
the demands of his father's debts on his shoulders, his
prospects did not look good. "Mr. Palmer, you have
your ear to the ground in the City, what rumours
abound regarding my estates?"

Palmer's face dropped, he leaned forward, "I
have been pressed by creditors seeking your
whereabouts, how long have your been in town?"

"Only yesterday, I came with Captain Quentin.
Do you know him?"

"Indeed sir, I wish I acted for him at the Prize
Court. He is an honourable gentleman."

Jonathan nodded his agreement, "I am fortunate
to have found his friendship, but what news of the
investigation into my father's death?"

"Sir Jonathan, I can only advise extreme caution.
As soon as you make yourself known to the
magistrates, or are seen at the offices of your father's
lawyer, bailiffs will be onto you. I have made discreet
inquiry; however, you will have to call at your bankers

to confirm the actual sums outstanding." He paused, putting his fist to his mouth and coughed. "Your father owed close to twelve thousand pounds and Westwood House is mortgaged for fifteen thousand."

Reality hit Jonathan with the speed of a canon ball flashing out of a fog bank, sudden, wounding, and leaving him feeling holed. All he had striven for during his twenty years of naval service was about to be wiped away by the foolish action of his father.

"And there is nothing left, not even the entail of my mother's fortune?"

"On that issue, you must consult your lawyer—it will depend on the entitlement of the original document."

Jonathan thanked Palmer and made to leave, but as he reached the door he turned back. "I can count on your integrity, sir?"

Palmer nodded. "Most certainly, Sir Jonathan, in my profession, my reputation must be as solid as Gibraltar."

* * * *

Jonathan's next interview with his bankers left a bitter taste in his mouth. They held the mortgage on Westwood House. Unless Sir Humphrey's estate settled the account by Michaelmas, the property would be put up for public auction. Convinced his situation could not worsen, Jonathan went to the

Lincoln Inn Fields office of his father's lawyer. The clerk took his details and asked him to wait.

The office comprised rooms in an ageing building with low ceilings, extensive dark oak panelling and a musty smell of damp pervaded the air, despite the warm August day. Eventually the lawyer emerged from the rear, a slender man, equal in height to Jonathan and not much older in years.

"Good day, Sir Jonathan." He extended his hand. "We have not met before. I took over the practice from my father last year when he fell ill. I am Henry Brook."

Jonathan took his hand. "My business is urgent, Mr. Brook. May we speak privately?"

"Most certainly, please this way." He led Jonathan into the next room, a small office filled with bundles of red-taped legal papers and heavy leather bound volumes. There was a small desk in the corner of the room, one chair behind and a single chair in front. "Please take a seat."

"Has probate been granted on my father's estate?" Jonathan asked.

Mr. Brook reached for a large bundle of papers, untied the red tape securing them, and started to sift through the documents. "No, Sir Jonathan, according to my records we have made no application at the court. I made note on reading of your father's demise to delay until I had instruction from his heir. You are he?"

"Yes I am."

"You will understand that I shall require signed affidavits from two gentlemen of standing to whom you have been known for at least seven years before I can proceed. It is a most unfortunate case. I have received several notes from creditors, all demanding payment in full, as always, and my firm holds no funds on behalf of the estate."

Jonathan watched him turn over documents as if he was looking for something in particular.

"I do have a copy of Sir Humphrey's will. He did not alter it when Mr. Westwood died." He looked up quickly, "Your brother...er...Jerome, did he marry?"

"No, despite regular complaint from my father, Jerome refused. He did not enjoy the best of health and lived mainly at Westwood House with our mother, whereas my father preferred town."

"Unfortunate that Sir Humphrey didn't remain more in country. In more ways than one, his life in town proved very costly."

"What is to be done?" Jonathan asked.

"Get the affidavits sworn, then I can put the case into probate. Do not pay any of your father's bills until we have a complete picture of the sums involved."

"What about the mortgage on Westwood House? The bankers will foreclose at Michaelmas."

Mr. Brook shook his head. "There is nothing to be done unless you have the funds, however, I would advise caution. You might settle Westwood House only to remortgage to keep the bailiff from your doors, then what sir? The Marshalsea?"

It was the first time Jonathan had thought of the consequences of unsettled debt. The prospect of the debtor's prison gutted him. He would rather go back to sea a pauper.

"Ah." Mr. Brook cried, "I have it." He pulled out a vellum document and unfolded it. It had a large seal embossed at the bottom. "Are you married sir?"

"I am not and from the news I have received this morning, I am relieved I do not have a wife and family dependent upon me."

"Wise words, sir, but this might be of interest to you and change your mind. It is the deed of entailment drawn up when your parents married. As the eldest son, you will inherit five thousand pounds when you marry and a further five thousand pounds when your first male heir is born. Were you aware of this arrangement?"

The news surprised Jonathan. "No, and I cannot recall either my mother or Jerome referring to the agreement. Perhaps it was a bone of contention between my father and brother, but I never heard of it. However, I have been at sea for a greater part of my adult life."

"Entailments are often of a peculiar nature. This was clearly done to preserve your mother's inheritance from your father. Aston Grange was also part of the agreement, but not entailed. Your father could do whatever he liked with the estate."

Jonathan straightened his back, "I believe my father was cheated out of that estate. It is my intention to claim it back."

"Then you must apply to the King's Bench, I can start to draw up the papers, but I shall need funds to commence the application, gather evidence, and prepare the case. I warn you, the whole business of disputed ownership can take years. Do you wish me to act for you?"

Jonathan thought for a few moments, he had his prize money, but how long would it last? "Start to prepare the case, I need the legal ground beneath my feet but going to law, Mr. Brook, I believe is a last resort."

"Well, Sir Jonathan, take a bride. Five thousand pounds will not settle your father's debts, but it will keep the bailiffs from your door, if you have a mind to marry, of course."

A pair of dark brown eyes gazing up at him flashed through Jonathan's head, he blinked to remove her image, but found his mental picture of Miss Ellis was not so easily erased.

"Now, the question of your father's death is another matter. The coroner in St. James' was informed and some inquiry made. However, because of the circumstances, a suicide verdict was brought."

The violence to his father on that ill-fated night quickly pushed Miss Ellis' lovely face to the back of his mind. "Mr. Brook, the pistol used to kill my father did not belong to him—all his weapons were adapted for the left hand. Whoever shot my father made the mistake of placing the weapon in his right hand."

Chapter Six

"An invitation to stay at Aston Grange, what an opportunity, you must make the most of it," Aunt Winters said to Catherine as they waited for Mrs. Quentin to arrive in her carriage.

"I am grateful you can spare me, but I do feel guilty about leaving you so soon after my arrival." In truth, Catherine was glad to get away, but she wanted to please her aunt who had been so kind to her. They stood near the window together, Catherine tall and slender, her aunt short and round.

"Guilty? Nonsense, my dear. Have you written to your mother and told her the good news? If not, I shall be only too happy to do so. I have an hour to spare before I call upon Mrs. Smith at the far end of High Street. She has been sewing for the poor and has promised me some children's clothes for distribution in the parish. Now, ensure Miss Roberts keeps a sharp lookout for your maid. Miss Cope is very young and Aston Grange has an all male staff. You don't want anything untoward happening during your visit, do you?"

Catherine knew her aunt's advice was given with the best intentions, "Most certainly not," she replied but felt there were times when good intent became overt interference.

At the first sound of a carriage, her aunt leapt up and opened the window. "There, I said Mrs. Quentin would be prompt, didn't I?" She rushed out to greet her and Catherine followed.

Mrs. Quentin, not having travelled far, didn't get down but leaned out of the carriage window. Catherine and her aunt dropped a customary curtsey to her, and she nodded back.

"Good day, Mrs. Winters, Miss Ellis. I am pleased to see you ready at the appointed time," Mrs. Quentin said. The lad riding on the box next to the driver had jumped down and held the horses, whilst the driver supervised the loading of Miss Ellis' luggage which had been brought out under Martha Cope's supervision.

"Good-bye Catherine. Enjoy yourself," Mrs. Winters called at the carriage moved off.

Inside the carriage, Mrs. Quentin and Catherine sat next to each other in the forward seats, and Miss Roberts and Miss Cope rode backwards. The conversation was polite as they made their way from the village and through the gates of Aston Grange. Catherine had heard much about the house and yearned for her first glimpse of it.

With its tall chimneys, she recognised the house style as late Tudor period, vertical mullion windows, horizontal transoms, and leaded glass. Instantly, she fell in love with it and could hardly wait to step inside.

As the carriage drew up outside the main entrance, Mrs. Quentin looked at each of the occupants in turn. "The Grange is staffed by former members of my husband's crew, thus, it may not seem like any other household you have experienced, however, should you have any complaint come to me directly. I am new to this establishment, too; however, let it not be said a house run like a ship is more efficient than a country home under the careful eye of its mistress." She paused as if waiting for reply, when none was made she said, "Come, the staff await our inspection and we must not disappoint them."

Taking Mrs. Quentin's lead, Catherine followed her. They were greeted by Mr. Sanders, who was introduced as the captain's former sail-master, and now Aston Grange's butler. The burly man standing before Catherine had a hook for his left hand. How would he manage his duties?

Sanders introduced the staff, who stepped forward in turn and doffed their caps to the ladies.

Catherine looked over her shoulder to ensure Martha was coping with the arrangements. It pleased her that her maid stood close to Miss Roberts, who had already been made known to the staff when Captain and Mrs. Quentin returned from their honeymoon.

Mrs. Quentin instructed Sanders to deal with Miss Ellis' baggage and invited her guest inside. Sanders escorted the maids upstairs.

"What a splendid house," Catherine said, awestruck by the height of the barrelled ceiling above and the sweeping oak staircase. Covered in dark oak panelling, the walls looked very formidable especially the pictures. A number of shadowy portraits, presumably of those who had lived in the house before, stared down at her.

Mrs. Quentin said, "I have no idea who those people are, I can only assume they are some of Sir Jonathan's ancestors. We must ask him when he returns, although I do think some of the gentlemen look a little dubious."

Still gazing up at the artwork as they ascended the stairs, Catherine said, "They do appear to be a rather a severe lot, although this lady is lovely." She pointed to a full length portrait hung at the turn on the stairs.

"I believe that is Lady Westwood, but we must ask Sir Jonathan when he returns." Mrs. Quentin smiled. "Sir Jonathan's mother was an heiress when she married Sir Humphrey, and Aston Grange was part of her dowry."

When they reached the upper floor, Catherine was shown to a suite of rooms in the guest wing. Her baggage had been placed on the large chest at the end of the tester bed. When Martha entered, Mrs. Quentin made to leave. "I shall go now and see what is planned for supper. Jackson, my husband's killick, who is in charge of the kitchen, has gone to London with his master, but I'm sure Sanders has made alternative arrangements for us to dine this evening. I'll leave you to your maid. When you are ready I shall be in the small parlour. Sanders will direct you. Then we can take a tour of the house."

* * * *

Later that same afternoon, three former navy officers were enjoying the taste of English beer at an Oxford Street ale house. "Your choice of establishment is not of the top notch, but the beer is good," Jonathan said.

"We must mark our steps carefully," Ross whispered. "Rumours are flying around town of your return. We can't be too careful. If Richmond's lackeys get onto us we must be prepared to take them on wherever we are."

"How can we be in danger? Richmond's a pompous ass who couldn't knock the skin off a rice pudding," Jeremy said.

"First unwritten rule of naval combat, do not underestimate the enemy," Ross said. "He is a cunning fox with a gang of paid henchmen around him. We know they stop at nothing—kidnap, murder...what more do you want?"

Jonathan took another swig of beer, wiped the froth from around his mouth, and stretched out his long legs. "Richmond, how do we find him?"

"Simple," Ross replied, "we set a trap and wait for him to come to us."

"But I do not understand." Jonathan leaned forward, "Why would he seek me out?"

"Richmond knows he got the Grange under false pretences—he cheated your father—why else was he so confident to offer him the chance to win the place back? He knew there was no possible risk involved. Your father was duped, lured outside, and murdered.

The whole episode was a set-up, and Richmond knew it from the start."

"Ross, we know this but how can it be proven?" Jonathan asked.

"Jackson's been making inquiries too." Ross smiled. "Let's say foraging in the less salubrious quarters. Richmond's real business is trade in young women—girls sometimes only thirteen or fourteen years old. His gangs steal them from the towns and countryside, wherever they can pick them up. He has merchantmen in his pocket. His innocent cargo of young women is ferried out to the French coast or round into the Mediterranean, and sold to pirates along the Barbary coast. Add trading in human slavery to his elicit gambling deals, plus his other fraudulent activities and you have the measure of the man."

"Do you have a plan Ross?" Jeremy asked.

"Yes, we do nothing."

"What?" the younger man cried. "How can we stand by and let a scoundrel like Richmond get away with...kidnapping and murder? He must be stopped and brought to book."

Ross brought his empty tankard of ale down on the table with a thud. "Be patient Jeremy, we must bait our trap. Richmond knows Sir Jonathan has returned. He will be aware of the inquiries made regarding Sir Humphrey's death and the inheritance. He will not favour involvement in a long legal battle."

Jonathan watched both men closely, but he felt like a beached whale, struggling on the sand in a foreign environment. Part of him wanted to go after Richmond alone, face him squarely, and fight him to the death. But what good would come of direct action? On land he had to obey the law; at sea, as captain, he was the law, as long as he followed the navy manual. "What is your plan?"

"I am convinced Richmond was behind your father's death. If I am right he will not hesitate to kill you. Return to the one place you can lure him to from strength—Aston Grange."

* * * *

Catherine changed her gown and left Martha to look after the remainder of the unpacking. She found Mrs. Quentin in a small parlour overlooking the garden.

"Miss Ellis, there you are," Mrs. Quentin said when Catherine entered the room. "Come over to the window and look at the formal garden. The outdoor staff must have worked exceptionally hard whilst my husband and I were away on honeymoon. They have transformed the beds, and the box has been clipped to perfection."

"What a delight," Catherine said as she gazed out of the window. Two gardeners were working not far from the house.

"Perhaps we could begin our tour in the garden; I can lend you a parasol." Mrs. Quentin rang the bell and the butler answered. "Sanders, Miss Ellis and I are about to take a turn in the garden. Could you bring us a parasol each from the hall?"

A few moments later, the ladies were strolling around the formal flower beds. "Mrs. Quentin, you must be very pleased with your new home."

"I wish I could say that I felt comfortable here, but it is not the case."

"Oh, dear, I am sorry if I have been impertinent. I did not wish to cause offence," Catherine said and followed her companion's gaze.

Mrs. Quentin was looking at a bench. She stopped and said, "Shall we take a seat?"

Catherine nodded her agreement and they sat down in a shaded corner. "This view of the back of the house is elegant. Often a house may have an excellent frontage and the rear appears most awkward. I am told there are streets of houses in Bath where great attention has been paid to the appearance of the houses when viewed from the front and little thought of elegance or design has been exercised at the rear. But as I have never been to Bath I cannot say with personal authority."

"I have been trying to persuade my step-mother to take the admiral there. I feel sure the waters would be excellent treatment for his injured leg, but Mary will have none of it. Please, Miss Ellis, as you will be painting my portrait and we shall be sitting together for some while over the next few days, could we not dispense with formality, at least in private. Call me Bella, if I may in turn address you as Catherine."

"Nothing could please me more. To be welcomed into your home is very generous of you, but to call you my friend is a privilege. I am much obliged, Bella."

"No Catherine, allow me on this occasion to feel the obliged."

They rose and, arm in arm, continued until they had completed the full square of the garden. Returning to the house the way they had left, they stepped through the floor-to-ceiling window, now fully raised, back into Bella's parlour.

"I shall ring for Sanders. He will enjoy showing us around as I am not fully cognisant with all of the rooms yet." Bella rang the bell.

Sanders entered. "You rang ma'am."

"Yes, Miss Ellis and I would like a fully guided tour of the house."

"Certainly ma'am," Sanders replied and opened the doors for them to step into the hall.

"Shall we start at the top of the house and work downwards," Bella suggested to the butler.

* * * *

Later that evening, as Jonathan and Ross dined with Jeremy at his club in St. James' a footman presented Jonathan with a note on a salver.

"By the Saints." Jonathan declared. "A note from a well-wisher says he's got important information concerning my father's death. What kind of an imbecile does the author of this communication take me for?" He waved the note in the air.

"A gullible one?" Ross replied. He leaned closer to Jonathan and said, "Now do you understand the need for expediency and diligence?"

Jonathan nodded. "So what do we do?"

Ross turned to Jeremy. "Can you arrange a room for us tonight here at the club?"

Jeremy frowned. "Of course, but why the sudden change? I thought you were putting up at Fladong's."

"We were, but surely that will be the first place Richmond's lackeys will look for a couple of ex-navy officers. If we stay here, we can make arrangements to return to Hampshire tomorrow." Ross looked at Jonathan. "If your business is concluded in London."

"Aye, I have put in motion all that can be done. I had little success at the magistrates and the constable of St. James' would look no further due to the coroner declaring a suicide verdict. I have instructed my lawyer to go to probate and to commence an action through the King's Bench regarding the ownership dispute. I have also been advised to lie low like some common criminal—much to my annoyance."

"Whatever for?" Jeremy asked his expression aghast.

"Debt." Jonathan let out long sigh. "My father's creditors will soon be at my heels after my prize money. But there was one piece of news which surprised me. According to my mother's marriage settlement, as the eldest surviving son, if I marry there's five thousand pounds, which my father could never get his hands on. Perhaps it explains why he was always pressurising Jerome to marry."

"Five thousand, eh?" Ross grinned and slapped Jonathan on the shoulder. "Looks like you're on your way to the leg shackles to join we happy band of married men."

Jonathan smiled. "I am not opposed to marriage, indeed I had considered the prospect during my voyage home, but I did not expect to find myself in such dire straits. I have no home to offer a bride. With the Peace in Europe, I have resigned my commission and am about to hide myself from creditors, who would strip me of what monies I have accrued like a plague of locusts. No sirs, I am not an eligible man."

"What utter nonsense." Jeremy said, "You, sir, have one extremely valuable asset—a title. My father-in-law refused me when I offered for Elizabeth, like you, I was a second son. My brother did not enjoy good health, when he died, the noble Glens sent their man of affairs to negotiate the settlement between Elizabeth and me. I can tell you, it stuck hard in the gullet. Had it not been for Ross reminding me that Elizabeth would have run off to Gretna with me when I had only my navy pay, I would not have realised how fortunate I was to have a love match. We were married with the Glen's approval. Now I am my father's heir, I dance to his tune not the hornpipe."

They brought their wine glasses together and toasted, "Marriage," in unison.

Jonathan looked down at the note he had cast on the table. "So what do I do about this?"

Ross fingered his dimpled chin. "Let's return it with a message stating you have just left."

Jonathan nodded and called a footman over to their table. "Return this to the man who delivered it, immediately. Tell him Sir Jonathan Westwood has just left the club." He reached into his waistcoat pocket and flipped a coin onto the man's salver.

"I've had a letter from Bella," Ross said, "she has gone to stay with the admiral and Lady Mary, but Richmond was sighted in Aston a few days ago."

"He's not had the audacity to turn up at Witton Abbey, has he?" Jeremy asked, "I thought the admiral had banned him from his land."

"The admiral did indeed," Ross replied, "however, the sighting took place outside the inn. It seems young Miss Ellis, who is Mr. Winters' niece and is staying at the parsonage, is an accomplished artist. She was sketching in the village and drew Richmond's likeness without knowing who he was. When Bella was leafing through Miss Ellis' sketch books, you can imagine her astonishment when she saw her cousin's likeness. The question is what has brought him out of town?"

Jeremy shrugged. "Business?"

"Aye. And we all know what sort of business he conducts near the south coast of England." Ross looked up as some disturbance from outside in the hall was attracting attention from the members. "What's going on?"

Jonathan looked in the same direction, towards the entrance hall of the club. A loud voice declared in a pompous tone, "Of course I can come in, I am a member."

"Talk of the devil." Jeremy whispered.

Jonathan straightened his back. He didn't want to stand and be too obvious after the warnings he had received during the day. A rotund gentleman, finely dressed in a tightly well-tailored coat, light breeches, and highly polished Hessians strode into the room. He had a broad face, short-cropped light brown hair and the highest pointed collar Jonathan had ever seen. His cravat was a cascade of flounces, the like of which he had only seen on the front of the gowns his mother used to wear when he was a child.

"Be Gads." Jeremy cried, "Richmond's got a cheek."

At that very moment Richmond turned towards them somewhat awkwardly, as if his head was welded to his shoulders. He squinted at them, then pushed aside a few members who had gathered around to see what the commotion was about, and strode towards them.

Richmond halted at their table. Neither Ross, Jeremy, nor Jonathan rose to acknowledge him. "Good evening, gentlemen," he said his upper lip curling as he spoke. When he received no reply, he continued, "Captain Quentin and Mr. Thwaite." He leaned forward in an awkward attempt at a bow, "I did not expect to see you in town at this time of year, thought you'd be gadding around following the sport now the shooting season is upon us." He switched his gaze to Jonathan. "I do not seem to have the acquaintance of your companion."

"And I sir, do not wish to have your acquaintance," Ross replied.

"Tut, tut, sir, this is no place for a display of bad manners, for are we not connected?"

"You know perfectly well we are, Richmond, but that does not mean I have to converse with you. I bid you good-night."

Richmond took the rebuff with an expression of disdain. He lifted his nose as if he had a bad smell beneath it. "Mr. Thwaite, I understand you, too, are not long in the leg-shackles. May I wish you happy?" He grinned "But should you wish to take advantage of your friend's hospitality at Aston Grange, I advise you do not delay. Captain Quentin is my tenant and will be gone from my estate by Lady Day."

Jonathan took the strong grip of Ross' hand on his wrist pressing him to the table as a signal to remain calm and not to rise to Richmond's provocation. With deep seated anger rising from his belly he said, "How dare you sir!"

"How dare I?" Richmond sneered. "I own the estate, sir, and if you had my acquaintance you would be aware of the fact. There have been significant changes in England of late, and my ownership of Aston Grange is one of them."

"You acquired the property by deception and fraud. Your claim would not have stood up in court if Sir Humphrey had not been conveniently murdered." Jonathan struggled against the restraining arms of his companions who kept him in his seat.

Richmond drew a lace-edged handkerchief from his sleeve and dabbed his nose. "A man would call you out for less, sir, but I am not one for duelling. The mere thought of spilling blood is truly offensive to my sensitivity. However, I assume I am addressing Sir Jonathan Westwood, although your ill-mannered companions have omitted to make the necessary introductions. My claim to ownership of Aston Grange is entirely above board. I won the estate fair and square from Sir Humphrey. That he should feel obliged to put a pistol to his head as a consequence, is not my affair. I bid you good-night, sir, and should our paths cross again, remember sir, I do not have your acquaintance, nor do I wish to have it." Richmond turned on his heel and strode across the room, where a crowd of people had gathered. They parted like curtains drawn aside as he passed through the throng.

"Calm down." Ross pressed his hand on Jonathan's shoulder. "That was merely the opening salvo."

"I should have called him out." Jonathan said.

"And what good would have come of it?" Ross replied. "I've told you, the chances of meeting Richmond on the duelling field are minimal. You would be cut down by his lackeys before you even got your feet on Wimbledon Common. He has no honour, he will never fight fair. Why do you think he came here tonight?"

Jonathan shook his head. Inside, he was a confusion of bewilderment, anger, and emotion. "I don't know."

"He wanted to come face to face with you. He knew you were here, he needed no formal introduction. Word would have reached him of your litigation regarding your counter-claim to the estate. Indeed, he would have taken great pleasure in spreading the news of your surfacing in town to every creditor within in a ten mile radius, if not further afield. Come, Jonathan, you and I must leave London at first light. If we hire good horses along the highway, we might make Aston before nightfall. Jeremy, how long do you plan to remain in town?"

"My father wants me to join his autumn shoot but I shall put him off as long as possible. I will remain in town for three or four weeks."

"Excellent old friend, then you can you keep us posted of any irregular movements regarding Granville Richmond, whilst we lie low at the Grange," Ross said.

Bound by a mixture of pain, grief and, hopelessness, Jonathan's reputation, honour, and integrity were placed in jeopardy. His temper riled, he wanted to fight Richmond. Although his friend's advice may not be the most honourable course of action, most certainly it was the wisest. "Thank you, gentlemen, for your comradeship when I most need it. Of late, every step I take appears to place me further from my goal." He looked at Ross and Jeremy in turn, "Do you ever feel life was simpler at sea?"

* * * *

Catherine added the final touches to a pastel portrait of Bella and stood back to examine the finished work.

"Am I done? There's someone I'd rather like you to meet." Bella said.

Intrigued, Catherine picked up her picture and turned it around for Bella to see. "There, do you like it?"

Bella gazed at the work. "I think you've flattered me, but I'm not complaining."

Catherine smiled. "As I explained when we started, this is only one of a few preliminary works I want to do. Once I have a feeling for your face and complexion, I'd like to do something perhaps in watercolour."

"Papa has a small collection of miniatures on ivory, can you work so small, Catherine, or do you prefer to work on a larger canvas?"

Catherine started to pack up her pastels. "I have tried a few miniatures, and will gladly attempt another, but I would prefer to work in oils. I hope you don't mind but I have already written home for my material to be sent. I would have brought them with me, but I didn't know whether I would have the room for them at the parsonage and my visit was arranged rather hurriedly."

"Yes, it must have been, for Mrs. Winters said nothing of you coming before the wedding and I am sure she would not have neglected to impart such an important piece of intelligence had she known it at the time." Bella got up from her seat and crossed the room towards Catherine's easel.

Catherine gazed at her as she approached. Her hostess most certainly had the measure of her aunt. "Mrs. Winters has treated me most kindly since I arrived and it was very good of her to take me on short notice."

Bella stood at Catherine's side. "Was there any reason why your visit was organised in haste, I do hope there is nothing wrong at home?"

Although Catherine had only known Bella for a few days she had instantly warmed to her and felt she could confide in her. "There were certain circumstances which my parents felt would be better resolved if I was absent from the neighbourhood for a while. You see..." she turned to face Bella, "I thought myself in love with Mr. Rossi, the art master my father had engaged to give me lessons. He came highly recommended and my artwork improved immeasurably under his guidance. Rossi was from Venice, spoke with a flowing Italian accent, and was the most interesting man I had ever met. Our friendship grew until one day he went down on his knees and begged me to marry him."

"But he hadn't sought your father's approval?"

Catherine sighed, "How did you guess?"

"I can tell from your tone that your story is not going to have a happy outcome. Come let's sit by the window."

When they had settled adjacent to each other on a window seat, Catherine continued, "He wanted me to elope to Gretna because he said my father would never allow us to marry, and upon that matter he spoke the truth. He told me how he had to make his living through his work, travelling up and down the country painting the portraits of the rich and their families in their country houses. He said I could go with him and paint the family groups, especially the children, such was my talent. Almost from the moment I could hold a brush or charcoal stick in my hand, I have wanted to be an artist. Papa will have none of it. I can paint for pleasure. I can sketch and draw my friends and people I see in the neighbourhood, but I must never advertise my artistic talents and offer to sell my work."

"So your engagement was kept a secret?"

"Yes, for a few days, then Rossi came up with a plan for us to run for Gretna—you see Bella, I have not yet reached my majority. I realised Papa would never give his consent, but asked Rossi to wait until January when I reached twenty-one."

"I don't suppose he was prepared to do that, was he?"

"How very perceptive of you, Bella. No he was not. Again and again he kept pressing me to pack my jewellery and leave with him. Always he asked me to

123

take my jewels. One of the servants must have heard him, perhaps, I don't know how Papa found out but I was summonsed one Sunday afternoon to my father's study. He told me he knew about us, he wasn't angry he said, but very disappointed in me. He didn't ask me what had happened between us but said I couldn't marry Rossi because he was already married."

Bella took Catherine's hand in hers, "Oh, what a terrible shock to have been deceived so."

Catherine hung her head low, "Yes it was, but to have my father believe I had been ruined by a married man, and that my hopes of an artistic life were shattered was overwhelming. I didn't try to convince him otherwise. I developed a melancholy ague and kept to my room. Of course, Rossi had gone when I emerged several days later, so I received no apology from him. I have no idea about his true feelings for me, except that he might have gone through a marriage ceremony and we could have lived happily as man and wife."

Bella squeezed Catherine's hand. "But for how long? Sooner or later, the truth would have emerged and you could have found yourself party to an illegal marriage. You did not go with him, but did he ever kiss you?"

Catherine felt a deep blush creep up her cheeks. She couldn't lie to Bella. "Once, in the orchard, under an apple tree, it was late May and the blossom was just lifting from the trees on the breeze. He proposed that day."

"And afterwards, when you had agreed to accept him, how many times did he kiss you?"

"He never kissed me again. We were in the house and there was always a maidservant or chaperone present when he came to give me art lessons. He used to write me notes and slip them to me."

"Did you ever write to him?"

"No, Mama was very strict in my upbringing. A young lady should never correspond with a gentleman, even if he writes to her, she always told me."

"Then you have nothing to reproach yourself for. Catherine, do not let this episode cloud the rest of your life. Rossi deceived you, I do not know what his motive was, and perhaps you will never know, but do not let him ruin the rest of your life. Your reputation has not been sullied. You have not been ruined, whatever your father might believe. You have a remarkable talent. You should not allow your fine gift to go to waste."

Catherine raised her head and took Bella's hand in both of hers. "Thank you for being my friend. I promise your portrait will be my finest work."

"Let us make it so. Now, do you remember I had someone I wanted you to meet, I have not forgotten. Do you ride?"

Catherine shook her head, "No I do not—we only had carriage horses in our stables."

"Well, I have a surprise. My father sent my horse, Merriweather, over today and I am most anxious to see her. I am hoping she is in foal. Shall we walk over to the stables and see if the mare has arrived?"

Chapter Seven

After breakfast the next day, Catherine stood before the cheval mirror wearing one of Bella's riding habits. Martha hovered behind her, adjusting the folds of the skirt. "I do hope I'm not going to regret this venture."

"But you look so elegant, miss," Martha said. "I hope you didn't mind me asking Miss Roberts for advice on the care of the garment and the correct way it should be worn, but I've not seen a riding habit before."

"I am very pleased that you sought her advice, Martha, it is the only way to learn. I am sure she was most helpful. How are you progressing with the set of letters I gave you?"

Martha smiled into the mirror at Catherine. "I have them all by heart and I can do the outlines on my slate."

"And have you copied out those lines I gave you using quill and ink?"

"Oh, yes, miss. Mr. Sanders has been most kind. When he saw me writing yesterday, he brought a slope and said I could use it for as long as we were staying at the Grange. I have it in my room."

"Good, then you must practise today whilst I am at Witton Abbey with Mrs. Quentin, although I wish I felt more confident about riding. I tried to explain to Mrs. Quentin yesterday that I had never ridden before. But she would have none of it and insisted I would be fine on a quiet mare. My fear is that the horse may decide to trot, or worse, gallop because I have no notion of how to stop the animal." Catherine turned to admire the cut of the jacket in the mirror. "I do like the silver buttons and military-style epaulettes." She touched the deep cuffs, edged with silver braid. "But I have reservations about the high collar and lapels."

Martha held out the hat and veil. "Miss Roberts says I must ensure the hat is securely tied with the ribbons, and also to use a few long pins." She placed it on Catherine's head at an angle.

"Are you sure this is how it should be worn?" Catherine asked.

"Oh, yes, miss. I tried the hat on under Miss Roberts' supervision." She secured the black silk hat, and brought the veil over Catherine's face. Finally she handed her mistress the gloves and riding crop.

Catherine paused, fully dressed in front of the mirror for one last glance. "I do hope I don't regret this."

As she descended the stairs, Bella, also wearing a riding habit, called to her from below, "Catherine you look every bit the part, I'd scarce take you for a novice."

"I wish I shared your confidence." Catherine crossed the hall, her emotions a mixture of anxiety and excitement. "I hope I'm not going fall off."

"Nonsense, I have the perfect mount for you, she is quiet and very biddable." Bella picked up her gloves and riding crop from the hall table and led the way out to the stables by way of the kitchen.

As they passed through the servants' hall, the men rose and doffed their caps. Bella turned to the butler, who was holding open the large door to the yard. "Sanders, we shall take refreshment with the admiral and Lady Mary, so there is no need to prepare a large meal. We shall return around six o'clock, if there is any change, I shall send word."

"Very well ma'am."

Catherine found the make-up of the Aston Grange household bewildering, although she could understand how the roles of the male servants had been allocated who took on the housekeeping responsibilities. Bella had brought her own lady's maid, Miss Roberts, but did Captain Quentin have men as house, scullery, and laundry maids? Heat flooded her cheeks at the prospect of her unmentionables being washed by a man. She made a mental note to ask Martha to take sole responsibility for any cleaning of her clothes in the next few days.

"I am so pleased you agreed to stay with me, Catherine, although I could have ridden out by myself with a groom, it is the companionship whilst riding I have come to miss. Captain Quentin appreciates my love of riding and has indulged me, possibly too much. His father, Colonel Quentin, has a fine stable and has begun his own stud."

"Do they live in the county?"

"No, we spent a part of our honeymoon with them in the Midlands, but the captain was also anxious to see some of the other developments in that part of the country. I have seen the Soho Works in Birmingham and the gas lighting in front, the vast furnaces in Shropshire, and Mr. Telford's iron bridge. However, I thought our visit to Worcestershire the most interesting because I was allowed to order a new dinner service from the factory. I am greatly looking forward to receiving the consignment."

"Isn't Sir Jonathan's ancestral home in Worcestershire?" As quickly as she had asked the question, Catherine wished she hadn't. She pressed her lips together and hoped her cheeks weren't developing a rosy glow.

As they turned the corner into the yard, Merriweather stood waiting with a stable boy holding her reigns. Bella began caressing the horse's head, so she didn't reply to the question. For a few moments, Catherine thought she hadn't heard her—but her relief was short-lved.

"We did make inquiries about Westwood House. A local innkeeper said the house had been closed up for some while. However, knowing my curious nature, Captain Quentin obliged me and we took a look from a distance. The house is situated on rising ground and encircled with masses of trees. It is brick built with stone quoins and parapets, and there is a gate-house immediately in front of the house. The gates are ornamented with the heraldic bearings of the Westwood family. I believe the family have lived there for many centuries."

On hearing about Sir Jonathan's home, Catherine's heart sank. If he belonged to a noble line of descent then he would be anxious to continue it. And as her father often reminded her, nobility marries nobility. She must not hope. But what harm could come from admiring the gentleman from afar?

Bella called to the stable boy who brought out another mare saddled like Merriweather. She turned to Catherine, "Watch how I mount and see if you can do likewise."

With the aid of a groom, Bella got into the saddle, fitted her left foot into the stirrup, and placed her right leg around the curved pommel. "Now it's your turn."

Catherine took a deep breath, placed her booted foot into the hands of the groom, grabbed the saddle, and sprang up.

"Bravo!" Bella cried. "I'll make a horsewoman of you yet."

Catherine wasn't so certain. Gingerly, she took the reins, holding them in her left hand as Bella had shown her, and her whip in her right. The mare shook her head. The movement gave her a start and she glared at Bella.

"Don't worry, we shall go at walking pace and the boy will lead your mount. Two grooms will accompany us. It's only five miles to Witton."

Five miles riding a horse for the first time sounded a very long way to Catherine.

* * * *

Jonathan and Ross had made good time along the London to Portsmouth road, changing horses regularly. Ross' man, Jackson, rode ahead and arranged for fresh horses to be available at each nominated coaching inn. At mid-day the captains stopped for refreshment and ordered beef stew with tankards of ale to be served in a quiet corner of an inn, away from prying eyes.

"Running from town does not sit easily with me, "Jonathan confessed.

"Aye, I understand," Ross replied, "but faced with uncertain odds at sea, you wouldn't turn your vessel and take a broadside if you had half a chance to outrun your enemy, would you?"

Jonathan smiled. "Put in those terms, no, but I am duty-bound to settle my father's debts."

"And that will put you into dun territory?"

"Yes, and the bulk of my money is still caught up at the Admiralty Prize Court, however, I have insufficient funds to settle the mortgage on Westwood House before the foreclosure at Michaelmas."

"Is it the loss of Westwood that hangs heaviest?" Ross asked.

"In many ways, my family have lived there for centuries, even Cromwell didn't succeed in ousting them, and now? I feel as blue as megrim."

Ross wiped his mouth with the back of his hand. "Don't get in a dudgeon, you know who your enemy is, you've seen the whites of his eyes. But do not underestimate him he will never fight fair, so you must always be two or three steps ahead. We will make the Grange our stronghold and, from what I know of the high-in-the-step Richmond, he won't like you in residence there."

"I am grateful for your help, but why are you putting yourself out for me?" Jonathan looked at his companion, trying to understand Ross' motivation. "Is there something you haven't told me?"

Ross scratched the dimple in his chin, as if deep in thought, before looking back at his companion. "What I am about to impart is to be kept in the strictest confidence. I am talking about revenge and that can be a bitter pill."

Jonathan leaned forward. "You have my word that anything you say will go no further."

"My desire for justice is a personal one," Ross said. "Various suspicious incidents have occurred around Aston in the past few months. The admiral's broken leg was no accident, his horse was shot by a marksman possibly of French origin, and I believe Richmond hired the would-be assassin, but I have no proof. Bella was abducted, bundled aboard a French merchantman, and nearly drowned when the ship foundered. Again, I believe Richmond to be culpable but I have no proof. You ask me why I am putting myself out for you? My answer is simple. I want Richmond brought to justice for the injury and strife he has caused to those I hold most dear."

Jonathan saw the passion flare in Ross' eyes and took it as a measure of the man's feelings.. "Why does Richmond seek to injure his own family?"

"As the admiral's nearest male relative, he believes he should inherit. He tried to persuade Bella to marry him. When she refused, he found other ways to claim the Richmond estate."

"How? What did he do?"

"Please understand, this is merely speculation. Refused by Bella, he saw the opportunity to acquire the adjacent property. Bella and I had been seen in each other's company and rumours were rife in the neighbourhood of an imminent announcement. That was when Bella was abducted. The plan might have been a forced marriage in France, and when the admiral met with another convenient accident, Richmond would claim Witton as well."

"Is there no end to the man's dastardly crimes? What motivates him? Revenge or greed? Surely there must be some underlying reason to cause him to turn on his family?"

Ross shook his head. "Perhaps, but I am not concerned with his reasoning, only his actions. He has wronged my father-in-law, my wife, and you. I know he is guilty of other crimes too, that is why I stand with you, and together we shall bring Granville Richmond to book."

* * * *

The sight of Witton Abbey gladdened Catherine's heart. Although she had enjoyed her first venture on horseback, and they had covered the journey at a leisurely pace, she feared her body would be stiff once they dismounted. Bella led the way to the stable yard, where the head groom came out to greet her.

"Good-day, Mrs. Quentin." he bowed his head and signalled for a stable boy to hold Merriweather's bridle as he helped Bella dismount.

"Thank you Pride," Bella said. "Miss Ellis is to be congratulated, this is her first ride. Will you help her down?" Pride nodded and came alongside Catherine's mare.

Slowly Catherine eased her right leg from around the pommel, slipped her left leg out of the stirrup, and shifted her seat until she was sideways on the animal.

"If I might place my hands around your waist, miss, and if you would care to steady yourself by placing your hands upon my shoulders."

Catherine followed Pride's instructions and he lifted her down. She thanked him but no sooner did her feet touch the ground, than her joints stiffened and her legs ached. She gave Bella an anguished look as she took a few steps towards her.

"Are you feeling unwell?" Bella asked.

Catherine shook her head, "No, but I swear I ache in muscles I didn't know I had."

"Oh, dear, I hope I haven't put you off riding for life. Please, let me?" She placed a supportive hand at Catherine's elbow and assisted her across the yard.

"Not at all, I have long wanted to ride but the opportunity has not presented itself before. I am very grateful for the experience."

"Does your father ride?" Bella asked as they entered the garden.

The image of her father astride a horse struck Catherine as odd. Her father was in his seventy-second year and, although a very fit man for his advanced years, she could not visualise him on a horse. "No, he always uses his carriage when he visits the mill and his farms. He may have ridden in his youth, but has never spoken of it."

"And your mother?"

Again Catherine couldn't see her serene mother travelling by any other mode than the carriage. Her mother, a well-educated daughter of landed gentry, had found herself seeking employment as a governess when her father's entailed estate passed to a distant cousin. "We live in a small town where my father conducts his business interests; if we cannot use the carriage, we hire a vehicle."

"I would dearly miss the countryside if I were to remove to the town. I do not like London and have no desire to reside there. Look. Lady Mary is over there." Bella waved at her stepmother sitting in the corner of the garden with a book.

Lady Mary rose as her visitors approached. "Bella, Miss Ellis, how delightful to see you, but riding habits on a warm day like today?" She frowned.

"Catherine has never ridden before so I persuaded her to try a quiet mare," Bella replied.

"Did you indeed? Well I hope you enjoyed your equestrian venture, Miss Ellis, but be warned: Bella has some madcap ideas and she doesn't always temper action with caution."

"What utter nonsense Mary." Bella replied a broad smile creasing her face.

"Come let us go inside where it is cooler. Would you like some lemonade?" Lady Mary led her two visitors into the small parlour and rang the bell. When Middleton entered the room she ordered the refreshment.

"How is Papa?" Bella asked.

"His usual gruff self. He is in the library reading. The *Naval Chronicle* came this morning so he is intent on gleaning every snippet of news from cover to cover. Hence, I have left him in peace. However, I am sure he will join us for tea when he knows you are here. How are you finding the Grange, Miss Ellis?"

"Much to my satisfaction." Catherine smiled.

"And what progress on Bella's portrait?"

Before Catherine could answer, Bella intervened. "The preliminary pastel sketches are finished and I am extremely pleased with them. Catherine is a talented artist. I am hoping she will be able to begin on my oil painting soon."

Catherine felt a blush warm her cheeks. "Bella is very kind but I think she exaggerates my skill. I have sent to Lancashire for my equipment and materials, when they arrive I shall be able to begin. Bella is an excellent model and I am looking forward to starting the work."

Lady Mary nodded her approval. "And I shall look forward to seeing it. Now, I have news—" She stopped as the door opened and Middleton stepped into the room carrying a large tray. He placed it on the table in front of Lady Mary.

"Shall I pour the lemonade my lady?"

"No, Middleton, I will attend to it. That will be all, however, please inform the admiral that Mrs. Quentin is here and perhaps he would care to join us for tea around four o'clock."

"Yes, my lady." He bowed and left.

When the door closed behind him, Lady Mary continued. "My brother Lord Norton and his wife are coming to Penley for a few weeks. Lady Norton did not specify in her letter, however, as I no longer reside there, she thought it might be a pleasant change to bring the children for the last few weeks of the summer. They have been in London with their eldest, Venetia, who came out this Season. Unfortunately she didn't take. My sister-in-law said there were offers but they were quite unsuitable. They removed to their seat in Surrey but Venetia continues in the doldrums, hence a change of scene for all the family."

"What sort of girl is Lady Venetia?" Bella asked.

"She inherited the family red hair," Lady Mary fingered her own unruly mop and twisted wiry strands back under her lace cap, "but I should be the last person to speak of her bran face. Her features are small, her figure slender, and her stature tall, so physically there is much to recommend her. She can be headstrong and disobedient, another character trait

I recognise in myself. However, aunt and niece differ greatly when dealing with others. Venetia is selfish; she flies into a passion and loses her temper when she can't have her own way. I am surprised she received offers, but doubtless her mother will inform me of the details when I see her. Lady Norton has asked about our neighbourhood. She wants to know if there are any eligible gentlemen in the vicinity, and would it be appropriate to hold a ball at Penley to introduce Venetia to the county."

Catherine's heart skipped a beat. Sir Jonathan was eligible, but would he return to the neighbourhood?

* * * *

Jonathan and Ross turned off the turnpike road and took the lane to Aston Grange. Jackson rode with them on the last leg of their journey. As they entered the stable yard, a cheer went up from the captain's men. Ross grinned.

"A fine welcome, captain." Jonathan nodded, inwardly touched with a dash of envy. He appreciated the value of a loyal crew like his own on the *Grafton* he had left behind in the Caribbean.

Ross dismounted, handed the reins to one of his men, and strode over to a fine hunter being groomed. He patted the horse on the neck and caressed him. "I could have done with you today, Warrior."

"A fine mount," Jonathan said as he got down. "I'm no great judge of horseflesh, but even I can tell he's better than some we've ridden today. Ouch!" He winced as a sharp pain ran the length of his back the moment his feet touched the ground.

Ross turned towards Jonathan. "We need hot baths, nothing better for banishing the smell of horseflesh and relaxing aching limbs Come, let's go into the house." He led the way through the rear entrance, which led into the kitchen. Once inside, he called to Sanders, the butler, "Roll out two barrels, hot water and plenty of it. We are stiff from the saddle."

"Aye, aye, captain, at once." Sanders said acknowledging Sir Jonathan with a nod and signalling two menservants"

"And a couple of brandies while we wait," Ross ordered. The men rolled two large barrels into the centre of the kitchen and pails of hot water were carried from the boiler next to the fire. The tubs filled quickly.

Jonathan downed his drink, removed his coat, loosened his cravat, and called a man over to help pull off his boots. Meanwhile, Ross stripped off his clothes.

"You see the advantage of keeping an all male household?" Ross grinned at his companion.

"Indeed, I can never remember taking a bath in this kitchen, even as child." Jonathan laughed as he removed the last of his clothing and thrust his arm into the hot water to test the temperature. He was on the point of leaping into the barrel when he heard a female voice cry out, "Ross!" He whipped his head around and saw Mrs. Quentin and Miss Ellis standing in the doorway.

Together, Jonathan and Ross dived behind their barrels."What a wonderful surprise," Mrs. Quentin said, advancing into the kitchen, "I had no idea you would be home today."

Jonathan glared at Ross as they crouched behind their barrels.

Slowly Ross stood up. "Bella, I thought you were staying at Witton."

"I didn't know how long you would be away and I wanted to come here," she said, "and when I had the opportunity to invite Miss Ellis...Oh, Catherine."

Mrs. Quentin must have turned back towards her companion because Ross said, "Get in the tub, now!"

Without hesitation, Jonathan stood up and jumped into the hot water, sending a wave of water splashing over the stone floor. The hot water stung his skin and he let out a loud howl, as did Ross.

Bella glanced quickly over her shoulder and grabbed Miss Ellis' hands. "Cover your eyes!"

As she guided her companion across the room, past the two captains in their hot barrels of water she said, "Good-day gentlemen."

When the ladies had left, Ross turned to Jonathan. "My most humble apologies, I had no idea my wife would be here. I daresay I shall not hear the last of this."

"Do not worry on my behalf," Jonathan said, he blinked but couldn't remove the image of Miss Ellis' surprised face from his mind. Clearly they had embarrassed her with their bravado bathing, but seeing her again ignited a flame within him.

* * * *

Catherine changed her gown and, not wishing to come between husband and wife, decided to stroll in the formal garden. *A reunited married couple need time together.* But her thoughts did not dwell on the Quentins for long. The picture of Sir Jonathan wouldn't leave her, no matter how many times she tried to push it out of her mind. His broad muscular shoulders and slicked-back dark hair kept teasing her. She was rather pleased he hadn't had it cut in the shorter style favoured by the current fashion plates she had seen. There was something wildly attractive about his long wavy locks tied back, his broad chest dark with hair, and his long limbs. Captain Quentin had also been similarly disrobed, but she couldn't have described or drawn him if she had tried. Whilst she had been in the kitchen, she only had eyes for one man.

How long would he be in the neighbourhood? Would he attend the ball at Penley? Lady Mary had seemed convinced the Nortons were set upon having a ball. She had attended a few balls at the houses where her parents were received and, of course, the balls at the assembly rooms in her home town. But a ball at a grand house like Penley Court would surpass anything she had experienced according to her aunt's description of the house. The prospect excited her—until the name Venetia invaded her thoughts. A younger version of Lady Mary sprang to mind. Her heart sank. If Sir Jonathan did happen to be looking for a wife, then most certainly he would look to the gentry. The daughter of Lord and Lady Norton must be, by birth, a better marriage prospect than a Lancashire merchant's daughter.

She let her gaze wander around the garden. To be mistress of Aston Grange would be reward enough, but to be Lady Westwood—she could not allow herself to be tempted down a path she knew to be impossible, however attractive the prospect might appear.

* * * *

Sanders brought a fresh shirt and breeches into Jonathan's bed chamber. "Your coat has been pressed and your boots polished, sir. Supper will be served shortly, if you would like to wait in the great hall."

"Thank you." Jonathan dressed quickly in the cleaned garments and struggled into his boots. Since crossing the threshold at the Grange he had felt a mixture of homecoming and alienation. Not that Ross' welcome had been lacking in any way, nor had the staff treated him any differently from a normal guest in an English country house. But there was the nub of his problem, his status as a guest. The house was achingly familiar, yet it wasn't his anymore

From the window, he looked down and saw Miss Ellis walking in the garden, her parasol shading her face from the early evening sun. She wore a yellow gown and matching bonnet, her dark mahogany curls surrounding her face. If he were looking for a wife, she might be the sort of girl who would suit him, but what did he know of her family? Would they consider him suitable?

He tried to push the thought of her to the back of his mind, but found the task surprisingly difficult. Gazing down upon the formal garden below, how naturally she blended in with the surroundings, as if the house had opened its arms and welcomed her to its heart. He hoped and prayed one day he would feel nurtured in a similar way and he could call both the Grange and Westwood House his own again. And Miss Ellis?

Jonathan tore his gaze away from the window. He had to focus his mind on the current situation and devise a plan of action. Ross had invited him to stay at the Grange. But to be a guest in the house where he had spent most of his boyhood summers, sat uncomfortably with him. He had commenced litigation, but in his heart he knew if he had to wait for the courts to act on his behalf to reclaim his estate, he could reach old age before there was a final settlement and then it might not go in his favour.

No, he needed a plan for the next few weeks and a longer overall strategy. He collected together the lists of his father's creditors as notified to the bank:

Palmer, the Prize Agent, and Brooks, the lawyer. He knew he could settle some, but not all. Using pen and paper from the desk in this room, he began dividing the creditors into degrees of urgency. Small traders, family firms who supplied his father with the necessities of life and whose livelihoods depended on receiving money for the goods and services they had provided. The gambling debts were by far the largest in monetary terms. Carefully he made his own list and wrote the dates of promised settlement alongside. A decision was needed, most of the gentlemen listed were well-know members of the *ton* for the sake of their reputations it would be unlikely they would publically demand payment. Perhaps he could put them off?

The bank proved the most difficult problem to resolve—there were several outstanding loans and the mortgage on Westwood House. Each of the two estates held special memories for him. He had been born at Westwood and spent most of his boyhood summers at the Grange. Which was most important to him?

He let the quill slip from his fingers, ink splashed onto his paper and across the palm of his hand. He tried to wipe it away and the stain grew larger. Would that happen to his debts? What could he do?

Inspiration hit him, like wind filling the sails after weeks becalmed in the Doldrums. The only barrier standing between him and Westwood House was the mortgage. The estate was worth more than the mortgage held against it. The bank would put it up for auction in an attempt to recover the debt, but their concern was not its true value, only the value of the mortgage. Someone could acquire a bargain at his expense. How could he raise the funds?

He looked at the sheet of paper, blotted with ink. The figures were clear; he needed to settle the mortgage on Westwood House. If he had to subsequently remortgage it, then so be it. He would still have possession of his ancestral home. There was one major problem—he only had ten thousand from his prize money, he was light by five thousand pounds. He placed his elbows on the desk, interlinked his fingers, and rested his chin on his hands. He needed to marry by Michaelmas.

Chapter Eight

When Catherine entered the house from the garden, she ensured she avoided the kitchen. After a few wrong turns, she found the great hall. A large carved stone fireplace dominated one of the walls, and an ornate balustrade staircase led to the upper floors. Breathtakingly dramatic, she stood gazing up at the stags' heads mounted at the highest level, then her gaze drifted over the many portraits she had viewed earlier. As before, most looked stark and unfriendly. But one portrait caught her eye, a rather stern gentleman possibly from the reign of King Charles I. She climbed partway up the stairs to get a better look at the signature on the bottom but could not make it out.

"I am very grateful to that fellow."

Catherine swung around at the sound of Sir Jonathan's voice below. He had startled her but she was determined not to let it show. She breathed out slowly and tried to find a few precious moments of thinking time. But why did everything she wanted to say simply fly out of her head the moment he walked into a room? She turned back to the painting and peered at the signature again "Who is he?"

Sir Jonathan mounted the stairs until he was at her level. She felt his dark eyes ranging over her as if she was the subject of the portrait not the cavalier.

"Sir Julius Bartlett, one of my mother's ancestors. His portrait has been here for as long as I can remember. When my brother and I were young, my mother used to tell us stories of the Civil War. Originally, the Bartletts were royalists, but when Sir Julius inherited the estate in 1641, he supported Cromwell and fought with the Roundheads. So, Aston Grange did well to survive plunder by being on the right side at the right time."

"And what happened to Sir Julius when the Restoration came?"

A smile creased Sir Jonathan's face. "He was an old man by then and publically accepted the new king, but whether he acknowledged him privately, we shall probably never know. It can be difficult to truly know a man's thoughts."

"I see he is wearing the buff coat and plain collared shirt of a Puritan," Catherine said, "so I assume this was painted during the Commonwealth, which surprises me as few staunch supporters of the new order allowed themselves the luxury of having their portrait painted."

Sir Jonathan made a flamboyant bow to her. "Miss Ellis, I bow to your superior knowledge. Perhaps we should draw a lesson from Sir Julius?"

"In what manner?" she asked, finding herself relaxing in his company. "Choosing the right side before a battle or managing to stay on the winning one?"

He grinned, "Of course, Miss Ellis."

"Are most of the portraits your mother's family?"

"Yes," he nodded, "Aston Grange was part of my mother's settlement when she married my father. As the second son, it was going to be mine."

There was a degree of melancholy in his voice so she changed the direction of their conversation. "Do you have any other brothers and sisters?"

He shook his head. "There was only Jerome and me. Are there several more Miss Ellises at home?"

"No, I am an only child. My parents were of advanced age when they married. My mother is Mr. Winters' half-sister. She is several years his senior."

Was he simply being polite, asking about her family, because she could think of no other motive to engage his interest? However, she was given little time to pursue her thoughts as the Quentins emerged from their apartments on the first floor and descended the stairs together.

"I've asked Sanders to serve supper in the breakfast room. We are only four at table and can be quite cosy there," Bella said. "Sir Jonathan, perhaps you will escort me in to supper?"

He bowed to her. "The pleasure is mine."

As Bella took Sir Jonathan's arm, Catherine half-wished she could changed places with her.

"Miss Ellis, may I have the honour?" Captain Quentin smiled at her and offered her his arm.

* * * *

Sat opposite to Miss Ellis throughout supper, Jonathan stole a few glances at her. Would she suit him? An only child, her father may not wish to part with her, but he might be tempted by a title for his daughter. There would be very little money left by the time the mortgage on Westwood House was settled. But to pay to pay it off, he needed to find a wife.

He wished he knew more about her background. He needed someone he could confide in without arousing suspicion that he was considering her as the future Lady Westwood. He decided to speak to Ross after the ladies had withdrawn.

"Catherine has drawn the most wonderful pastel portrait of me." Mrs. Quentin said, "I shall have it framed and she has also promised me an oil painting, isn't that so?"

Although Miss Ellis smiled, Jonathan thought she wasn't comfortable having her talents publically acclaimed. He liked her sense of modesty, and on closer observation, was convinced there was no falsehood in her expression.

"I am hoping to begin when my materials arrive from Lancashire," Miss Ellis said.

Mrs. Quentin looked at her husband. "I explained an order could have been made up when you were in London, but Catherine would have none of it."

"I prefer to work with my own easel and brushes," she said, "I have a good selection of oil paints and it would have been an unnecessary expense to order more. It will only be a few days and I am sure they will be delivered safely."

Her response impressed Jonathan. It suggested economic frugality, and any wife of his would need to exercise that particular quality. "How long will it take to complete a portrait?" he asked.

She smiled. When her dark eyes looked directly into his and held them for a few seconds, his senses heightened and he leaned forwards. "Two to three weeks and then the painting will have to dry thoroughly. That could take longer, depending on the weather in September. If we have a dry autumn, the picture could be framed and hung by the beginning of October. However, I am not a professional, merely a very keen student who enjoys art."

"Will you be able to stay with us to complete the work?" Mrs. Quentin asked.

"I expected to stay a full six weeks at the parsonage. However, I shall write to my mother and see if she can spare me for a while longer, if that is agreeable to you, Bella?"

"Oh, most certainly, however, I do feel guilty depriving Mrs. Winters of your company." She glanced over the table to ensure everyone had finished eating. "If you will excuse us gentlemen?" She stood up and Miss Ellis followed.

Jonathan and Ross rose as the ladies withdrew. Ross signalled Jackson, who served at table instead of Sanders, "Brandy," he ordered, "and leave the decanter."

When they were private and Jonathan had finished his second glass, he put his plan to Ross. "I intend to settle the mortgage on Westwood House before Michaelmas. It is the only way I can secure the estate. If I allow the bank to foreclose, they will sell the property at auction and it could be lost to me forever."

"A sound plan," Ross replied, "but what about this place?" He waved his hands in the air.

"Of course, I want to regain ownership," Jonathan said, "but it might take time. I can't allow my ancestral home to slip through my fingers for want of the blunt. It pains me because I know I shall not be able to settle all of the debt and I may have to re-mortgage within a few months, but at least I have a fighting chance of recovering my inheritance."

"In your position, I would probably make the same decision. By now, news is about town of your ownership dispute with Richmond, he won't be able to sell and that will make his hackles rise. But be warned, he tried to have the admiral killed, and succeeded with your father, he won't hesitate to get a few lackeys to see you off. Once you're out of the way, there'll be no one to challenge him legally."

"Let's hope it won't come to that." Jonathan sighed.

"If it does, my friend, I promise you, I will avenge you, if I have to kill Richmond myself."

Jonathan stared at the amber liquid in his brandy glass, swirling it around the base before downing the entire contents. The liquid burnt the back of his throat and slithered down to his stomach. He looked back at Ross, his glass was empty too..

"Another, my friend?" Ross said.

Jonathan nodded and held out his glass. When he had taken another drink, he felt ready to raise the question of marriage. "Miss Ellis, what do you know of her?"

Ross smiled, "She is quite pretty, reasonable company as she doesn't talk too much, and when she does speak, what she says is worth listening to. That, my friend, is a rare commodity in a female."

"Yes...but what do you know about her family?"

He shrugged, "Not much. If you wish to know about them, I suggest you ask Bella. Doubtless she will ask Mrs. Winters, and then the whole parish will know, so you might as well offer for Miss Ellis tonight and save us all the trouble of speculation."

Jonathan laughed. "Am I so transparent?"

"I'm afraid there were a few moments over supper when your interest in the young lady was evident. But looks can deceive, how do you feel about her?"

Jonathan didn't answer. He lent back in his chair, put his hands behind his head, and gazed up at the ceiling. After a few moments, he groaned. "I have feelings for her, I'm attracted to her, but I hardly know her. If I were to make her an offer, how does she feel about me?"

"Take heart, my friend, we men are not good at expressing our true feelings. However, if it is any consolation, I can wholeheartedly recommend the honourable state of holy wedlock."

"I'm glad to hear it, but another matter is pressing on my conscience. I need my mother's entailment to settle before Michaelmas, otherwise I lose Westwood House. My conscience tells me to confess all to Miss Ellis and hope she will marry me, but part of me wants to woo her and win her genuine affection."

"Ah. I believe you have a tiger by the tail." Ross chuckled. "Oh, don't look so glum. I would woo her, but best not tell her about the money, women can be so prickly about matrimony. Of course, there is always the possibility she might turn you down."

Jonathan put his elbows on the table and cupped his chin in his hands. "I don't need to hear that, especially as it's just over a month to Michaelmas."

"Aye, and you'll need three weeks to get the banns read—and that's if her father agrees. How about getting a special licence, or you could make a run for Gretna?"

"I do hope you didn't feel embarrassed when we came upon the gentlemen in the kitchen earlier?" Bella asked as she sat sipping coffee in the drawing room.

Catherine raised her eyebrows. "It was an enlightening experience and an unexpected surprise, but I don't know who suffered the brunt of it. I'm sure it wasn't me."

Bella chuckled. "I asked Ross, but he thought the whole incident was highly amusing and laughed it off. I scolded him for doing so because Sir Jonathan didn't take it so lightly, and for the sake of decorum, I had to march you away with your eyes covered. They weren't expecting us to be here. I had planned to apologise to you, but we both needed to change from riding. As soon as I was dressed, Ross came into my chamber. We began to discuss his journey to London, and I quite forgot. Do forgive me; you must think I am the most dreadful chaperone."

"There is nothing to forgive." Catherine shrugged, especially as she had secretly admired her glimpse of male torso, but she didn't want to confess it to Bella. "Perhaps it is regular behaviour in the Royal Navy. We were not expected to be present, so maybe the onus is on us to apologise."

Bella frowned. "I think the least said about the bathing barrels, the better. We should concern ourselves with more important matters. If the earl and countess hold a ball to announce their arrival at Penley, it will cause much excitement in the neighbourhood."

"Really? Are there many balls held in the locality?"

Bella placed her cup and saucer on the table beside her chair. "Lady Mary held the last ball earlier this summer, before the weddings. The house at Penley isn't large but it has the most delightful ballroom. News had spread throughout the county about a naval captain of some fortune who had settled here. Hardly anyone turned down their invitation. It was quite a crush."

"Do you anticipate another ball to be so well attended?" Catherine asked, trying to suppress a mental image of Lady Venetia Norton. It was total conjecture because she had never met the earl's daughter.

"I would think so, few would turn down an invitation from Lord Norton—and there is his daughter, Lady Venetia. She may be feeling low, having not secured herself a husband in London; on the other hand, she may be grateful to escape unwanted suitors."

"Of course." Catherine sighed inwardly. "I hadn't considered an unsuccessful Season as a blessing."

"Do you want any more coffee? Or shall we have some entertainment before the gentlemen join us?"

"I can play, if you wish?" Catherine offered pointing to the instrument at the far end of the room.

"I do not recommend it." Bella's hand flew to her mouth. "Oh, I didn't mean to throw aspersion on your playing, but the instrument is badly out of tune. I don't think it has been played in years. I spoke to Ross about it when I tried to play a tune upon our arrival. It sounded dreadful."

"Shall I fetch my sketches, or do you play chess? I noticed a fine ivory and ebony set in the great hall."

Bella sat up, "Do you play chess?"

"Yes, my father taught me and he plays regularly at his club. I am an only child. When there are no sons at home, daughters must forsake their needlework for different pastimes. I love to play, although, be warned, I have been tutored by a strict master. I only play to win."

A broad grin creased Bella's face. "Catherine Ellis, you're a delight. We shall play, but on one condition, should the gentlemen join us, we must give up our game and pretend we haven't played. I have a little plan that will tease my husband and, I hope, intrigue Sir Jonathan." She rose and crossed the room to the door leading into the great hall.

What had she done? She played against her father regularly and the first time she had beaten him she was one month short of her fifteenth birthday. She had thought it would annoy him; on the contrary, he was very pleased with her and encouraged her to study the strategy of the game. But what would Bella expect of her?

She didn't have to wait long. Bella came back carrying a chess board and a wooden box. "Let us set up the chessmen over there." She put the box down, opened the board and began setting out the pieces. When Catherine sat down, most of the pieces were in their positions.

"Which hand?" Bella asked, putting her arms behind her.

"Er..left," Catherine called and smiled when she discovered she would have the first move.

"Let's see who luck favours tonight," Bella said.

Catherine used a standard opening, moving her pawn. Bella responded, thus setting the pattern of their game. Catherine tried a few ploys she had used successfully when playing her father, but Bella read the move and defended against further action. "You play a very defensive game," she said at length, hoping her comment might distract her opponent.

Bella smiled as she placed her fingers on her queen. "And, Miss Ellis, I see you use all your powers of diversion to cause your opponent to falter." She picked up the piece and was about to place it down when the sound of male voices in the hall stopped her. "Shall we declare this a draw?"

"Agreed." Catherine nodded.

"Quick. Let's reset the board for the gentlemen."

A few moments later, the double doors were opened by Sanders, and Sir Jonathan and Captain Quentin entered the room in deep conversion with each other. Catherine pressed her lips together, determined to speak only when spoken to.

"Coffee gentlemen?" Both men agreed on a cup and Bella instructed Sanders to bring a fresh pot. "I thought we might have some music after supper, but when Miss Ellis offered to play I remembered the pianoforte needed attention."

Catherine tried not to look at Sir Jonathan, but she couldn't resist a quick glance in his direction from time to time.

"What a pity," he said sitting down. "My mother was very fond of the instrument and played tolerably well."

"I'm sure it can be restored once we have engaged a suitable tuner from Portsmouth," Bella replied, "however, in the absence of music, how about a game of chess?"

Catherine stole another glance, the nerves at the base of her spine tingling. Sir Jonathan didn't look too perturbed about the suggestion. Perhaps he was a regular player, too? Next she glanced at Captain Quentin, resting his chin on his hand. He looked as though he was suppressing mirth. What was Bella's little plan?

"Sir Jonathan, do you play?" Bella asked.

"It has been known, yes, sometimes when we have been at sea for many weeks. A game of chess engages the mind, allows one a certain measure of circumspection, and teaches caution, or not to make moves too hastily. I regarded chess as a useful deployment on the *Grafton,* especially as training for the mid-shipmen."

"But have you ever played a member of the fairer sex?" Captain Quentin asked, "because I believe my wife has a tournament in mind for us."

"A tournament?" Sir Jonathan coughed. "I doubt if my game is of sufficient calibre. I play only for amusement."

"And that is all we shall be doing, now come gentlemen," Bella urged, "if Catherine plays against you, Ross, for I know you do not want to play against me, and I play Sir Jonathan, then the winners can challenge each other? How does that sound?"

Catherine had remained silent but had reservations. Bella was about to pit her against the captain and she had no idea what sort of player he was. If he was good, she wouldn't mind losing to him. But if his game did not challenge her, she had no intention of letting him off lightly. She had been schooled to play to win, and she intended to play her best game. But what would Sir Jonathan think of her?

"Come, come," Bella urged, taking her hand and leading her to the small table. A flutter of butterflies quivered in her stomach. She took a deep breath and tried to remember the stock defences to most opening gambits as she sat down.

Captain Quentin stood up, sauntered across the room, glared at his wife, and said, "What are you up to?"

"Just a bit of amusement," she replied, "now which hand? Catherine would you like to choose?"

"Left," Catherine replied, certain that Bella would be holding the chess piece in the same hand as before.

When Bella opened her left hand it was empty. "You have the advantage Ross. Do you wish to play white?"

He nodded and opened the game with the standard pawn gambit."Do you play chess often, Miss Ellis?"

Catherine replied with her opposite pawn before looking across the board at him. "Yes, my father taught me, I told your wife earlier." She saw a sparkle of recognition in his dark navy eyes as he glanced across the room at Bella before returning his attention to the game.

Playing black, Catherine adopted a defensive game, meeting each of his challenges with a back-up piece, until she swung to the offensive by taking the white queen.

"Bravo." Bella applauded. "Excellent move."

"I deserved that Miss Ellis, caught with my defences down, I should have seen that coming. Perhaps you understand now why I do not play against Bella. I believe you play a similar game and take no prisoners."

"I play as well as I can. The way my father taught me," Catherine said.

Throughout the play, she was aware of Sir Jonathan standing a few paces away. He had his arms folded in front of his chest and his long eyelashes hooded his dark eyes. She took brief glimpses of him—she needed to concentrate on the game. The very last thing she wanted to do was play badly.

"Your move, Miss Ellis," Captain Quentin said, placing his empty coffee cup and saucer on the table.

Catherine blinked "No sir, it is your move."

"Strange, I could have sworn I moved my bishop."

"You did, Ross," Sir Jonathan said, "but Miss Ellis has replied with her queen's knight."

"Oh, dear." The captain placed his elbows on the table, cradling his chin in his hands. "This doesn't look good." He moved a pawn to attack the knight but the defence was too late, he had left an opening. Catherine moved in for the kill.

"Check," she said.

Her opponent scanned the board. "Don't you mean checkmate, Miss Ellis?"

"Yes, Captain Quentin, I'm afraid I do."

"Come, Sir Jonathan, it is our turn. Shall we sit?" Bella pointed to the vacated seats, Are you ready, Sir Jonathan?"

He nodded and the game began. Catherine took up position behind Bella's right shoulder, anxious to see the run of play from Bella's position. It was evident from the opening that he was no match for her. Although he defended well, he made few positive moves—all were reacting to the growing pressure mounted on the black king by Bella. Eventually, he tipped over his king.

"Forced to haul down your colours, eh?" Captain Quentin said as he glanced over the board, a smile hovering around the corners of his mouth. "Perhaps now you understand why I don't play chess against my wife." he smiled at her.

"You could have forewarned me," Sir Jonathan said.

"And ruined my amusement," Captain Quentin replied. "Come, join me in a drink Jonathan, there's nothing better to wash down bitter tasting coffee than a tot of rum." Captain Quentin led Sir Jonathan to the far side of the room where he filled two small glasses with a dark amber liquid.

"It seems we have been abandoned to our game. Would you like to do the draw?" Bella said.

Catherine picked up a white pawn and secreted it in her hand. Only half-listening, she couldn't remember which one Bella had chosen, so she opened both. Much to her surprise she had won white and, thus, the first move. She opened the game with a standard gambit, remembering how Bella shadowed her moves before. They played several moves in silence, trading pieces, until Catherine decided to switch the balance of the game. Instead of giving Bella a piece to move against, she selected an apparently non-threatening move.

Bella frowned and took another of the black pawns. "I do hope you are playing to win and not dealing me false."

Catherine made another move based on the strategy she had fixed in her mind. She hoped Bella wouldn't see her disguised attack until it was too late. "Be assured I am playing to win."

Bella took a black bishop with her queen. "Good, although I am a little disappointed we have been abandoned by the gentleman."

Catherine followed Bella's eyes across the room to where the gentlemen were seated together deep in conversation. She glanced back at the chessboard and moved her queen's rook. Silently she watched her opponent pick up her queen's knight. Bella had fallen into the trap. "I do not think either of them wanted to play, they agreed to please you."

"The gentlemen should have more sense, especially my husband. I thought he would understand my character now we are married." Bella placed the knight back on the chessboard.

"I think both he and Sir Jonathan have much on their minds and must be fatigued from their journey." Catherine moved her queen. "Check."

Bella's eyes widened, "How could I possibly have fallen for...?"

Catherine smiled, "Concentration or fatigue?"

"Or simply bad play. Congratulations, Catherine. I am rarely beaten but you are a worthy opponent. Perhaps we can play again when we have fewer distractions?" Her eyes shifted to the direction of the gentlemen. "Do you think they have noticed?"

Chapter Nine

The next morning Catherine looked out of the drawing room window and saw her uncle's carriage coming down the driveway. "I believe you have a visitor, Bella, Mr. Winters' carriage has drawn up outside and my aunt is descending."

Bella put her book down. "Does she look as though she is in a hurry?"

Catherine nodded. "I believe there is some urgency in her gait."

"Then prepare yourself, because I suspect Mrs. Winters has urgent news of Penley. Indulge her Catherine, she is a good-hearted woman, but she does so like to be first with the news. Do not steal her thunder by telling her we already know Lord Norton is coming to the neighbourhood and there's to be ball, agreed?"

"Of course, she may know when they are due."

Sanders opened the doors and announced Mrs. Winters, who hurried into the room looking flushed.

"Good day, Mrs. Winters," Bella said, "please, won't you join us?"

"Thank you Mrs. Quentin, I hope I find you in good health and Catherine, my dear, you are looking very well." She eyed the butler, when they were private she said, "I have the most exciting news about Penley Court. More than we could possibly have hoped for. The Earl and Countess are coming to stay for a few weeks. They are expected within the next few days. There has been considerable upheaval in the village, stores have been ordered and the butcher has received a long order. Everyone is very excited. Can you imagine what an honour it is for the neighbourhood to have nobility residing in our midst?"

"That is good news indeed, Mrs. Winters," Bella said "Are they expected in the next few days?"

"Absolutely, I heard it from the butcher and Mrs. Ward, the housekeeper, only this morning and there is more." She clapped her hands together. "There is to be another ball at Penley. Of course, you were not in the neighbourhood for Lady Mary's summer ball, Catherine, but it was a very grand occasion and attended by half the county. Goodness knows what other important families will descend upon the parish once Lord and Lady Norton are in residence."

Guilt ran through Catherine's veins. She didn't like deceiving her aunt and felt she should say something. "Are other members of the Norton family accompanying the earl?"

"Oh, yes, my dear, they are bringing all of their children, and the governess, maids and so on. Their household totals quite a number of servants, I understand. My special news concerns their eldest daughter, Lady Venetia, who is reputed to be quite a beauty. She will be with them, as they are coming direct from London."

"Venetia, what a lovely name," Catherine said, glancing at Bella. Lady Mary had described her niece's character but said little of her looks.

"I suspect the earl and countess visited Venice on their honeymoon," her aunt added, "as the daughter was their first born. Oh, they have several boys, too. Now Lady Venetia has just had her first London Season, but she doesn't seem to have taken, so they are coming into Hampshire."

A slight frown creased Bella's forehead, "I do not follow, Mrs. Winters, how is Lady Venetia's Season related to Hampshire?"

"Well, Sir Jonathan is here, isn't he?"

Catherine tensed, her stomach fluttered, and she bit her bottom lip. She hoped her reaction to his name would go unnoticed, but her curiosity had been aroused. "How do you know?"

"It's all over the village. Mr. Winters rushed back from his morning prayers to tell me Sir Jonathan and Captain Quentin arrived home yesterday." She looked at Bella and smiled. "I'm sure you are most pleased to have the captain home, Mrs. Quentin."

"Of course, Mrs. Winters, and surprised the news about my husband's homecoming has spread so quickly."

"Blame Huggins, the innkeeper, the man is the most notorious gossip. Where he gets his information from, I have no idea—servants, stable lads, and the carriers who regularly use his hostelry maybe."

Did the inhabitants of Aston have little better to do than amuse themselves on the comings and goings of their neighbours?

"You mentioned a ball, didn't you Mrs. Winters, at Penley?" Bella asked.

"Why yes, I could hardly curb my excitement. It is to introduce Lady Venetia to the county, a sort of coming-out, but nothing like the scale of her London one. I suppose Lady Norton might have Sir Jonathan in mind, although, as an earl's daughter someone higher in the *ton* might suit better. However, in the short time he stayed with us, I was particularly taken with Sir Jonathan's good manners, conduct, and melodious tenor voice. Why I only have to close my eyes when I am sitting in my best parlour and I can hear him singing *Heart of Oak* accompanied by Catherine on the pianoforte, such was the impression left on my memory."

"Who told you about the ball, Mrs. Winters, and how do you know it is certain?" Bella asked.

"I spoke to the Penley housekeeper this morning. She received instruction from her mistress to prepare the house not only for the family but also for a large party of visitors. And she told me the date for the ball has been set for the twenty-eighth of this month."

* * * *

Jonathan and Ross rode towards the long meadow between the turnpike road and Aston Hill.

"Over there," Ross called as he pointed to the drainage ditch his men had dug. "It was quite a challenge, but you know how it is—men thrive on work. When the rain comes in the autumn, hopefully, this meadow won't turn into a quagmire."

They followed the length of the newly dug ditch and entered the woods at the base of the hill. As they passed through the woodland, they slowed to a walk and had to duck to avoid low branches along the way.

"Can I ask your advice on a delicate matter?" Jonathan said.

Ross nodded. "You can ask, and I will endeavour to give my best advice, but you may choose to ignore it. What's this delicate matter? Miss Ellis?"

Jonathan nodded. "If I were to make her an offer, do you think I would be received favourably?"

"How do I know? I'm the last person to give advice on matrimonial matters. Why, I made the most dreadful hash when I first proposed to Bella. Jeremy tried to put me right, but I was so angry when she turned me down, I couldn't think straight. Apparently, I didn't woo her sufficiently and tell her how much I admired and loved her. I remember Jeremy taking me heavily to task on my lack of understanding of females."

"But, obviously she did accept you in the end."

Ross chuckled. "Aye, but that is—" He reined in his horse.

"What's wrong?" Jonathan called over his shoulder, drawing his mount to a halt.

"Shhh." Ross brought his forefinger to his mouth. "What can you hear?"

Jonathan strained his ears, listening for the faintest sound. He looked back at his companion. "Nothing."

"Exactly, no birdsong, nothing, I don't think we're alone." The words were hardly out of Ross' mouth when a shot rang out.

Jonathan heard a loud explosion erupt inside his head as if his eardrums had exploded. He slumped forward into blackness.

* * * *

Catherine added the finishing touches to her watercolour. She stood back, pleased with her work and the way she had captured Sir Jonathan's likeness. The pounding of a horse's hooves ridden at full gallop towards the house brought her to the library window. It was Captain Quentin astride a powerful hunter leading another horse with the body of a man tied across the saddle. Her heart pounded and fear gripped her insides—the man across the horse looked like Sir Jonathan. She rushed into the hall.

Sanders had opened the door wide and menservants seemed to pour through the entrance from all directions, all eager to help lift Sir Jonathan down from his mount.

"What's happened?" Catherine cried, her nerves tingling, her head beginning to spin, she clenched her fists and started to chew on her forefinger.

"He's been wounded," Captain Quentin called over his shoulder as he struggled to release the leather ties he had used to keep Jonathan across the saddle. "I think a musket ball grazed his skull, but he breathes and his heartbeat is steady. Sanders, Jackson, Dixon, McCoy help me carry him upstairs to his chamber."

"I'll fetch Bella," Catherine called, but doubted if the captain heard her. She ran upstairs, mounting the stairs as fast as she could. Loudly, she knocked on Bella's bedroom door.

The door opened and Miss Roberts stood barring the way. "Mrs. Quentin is resting," she said in hushed whisper, "and is not to be disturbed."

"She will want to hear this," Catherine said firmly as she stepped into the room and pushed her way past the maidservant.

Bella, who was lying fully dressed on top of the bed, raised her head from the pillow. "What's wrong Catherine?"

"There's been an accident. Sir Jonathan has been wounded in the head. He's unconscious."

"Help me up," Bella called to her maid and tried to sit up. She took a gulp of air, sank back onto her pillow, and let out a long sigh.

"Are you unwell?" Catherine advanced to the edge of the bed. Miss Roberts was fussing around her mistress on the other side.

"I have been feeling a little nauseous of late, it is nothing. It will soon pass, but Sir Jonathan, what sort of accident?"

"Captain Quentin wasn't specific. The men are carrying him to his bed chamber."

Bella sat up, swung her legs to the edge of the bed. The maid leant towards her, offering her a hand.

"I'm fine, please don't fuss. Roberts, bring me my shawl."

Bella's complexion had paled. The bloom Catherine had painted in the portrait of her a few days before had drained from Bella's cheeks.

Catherine strode back to the door and opened it Outside, men were waiting on the landing of Sir Jonathan's room, the door of which stood open. She peered inside, but could only see the back of Captain Quentin's broad shoulders standing over the bed where she assumed Sir Jonathan had been put.

"Has Dr. Grey been sent for?" Bella asked.

Catherine turned towards her. "I don't know."

Bella walked into the bed chamber. Catherine wanted to follow, but propriety forced her to keep a modest distance. As much as she yearned to be at Sir Jonathan's side, she knew she had no right to invade his privacy. She heard Bella ask her husband if medical assistance had been sent for. He replied that a rider was already on his way to Portsmouth to fetch Dr. Grey.

"Is he seriously injured?" Bella asked.

Captain Quentin shrugged, "A musket ball scraped the top of his head and as he slumped forward he might have hit his head on a branch. He's lucky, an inch lower and he would have had his brains blown out."

"Oh, Ross." Bella sighed. "Is this horrible business starting all over again?"

* * * *

It was early evening when Dr. Grey arrived at Aston Grange in his curricle. He went immediately to his patient, who had not recovered consciousness. Catherine and Bella waited downstairs in the drawing room, whilst Captain Quentin accompanied him.

Catherine, shocked by Sir Jonathan's accident, was also concerned about Bella. However, by the time the doctor had arrived, Bella had recovered some of her colour. As they took tea and waited for further news, Catherine wanted to ask about the comment Bella had made earlier to Captain Quentin, but she felt she was being most impolite to probe. But fear that something ominous was about to occur would not subside. After a couple of hours of inner struggle, she could contain herself no longer.

"Bella, I hope you do not mind me asking but I overheard you saying something about this horrible business starting all over again, what did you mean?"

Bella put her teacup down. "It appears that someone took at shot at Sir Jonathan, obviously with the intention of killing him. In the spring a similar *accident* happened to my father. Someone fired at him whilst he was about his estate. His horse was brought down and my father broke his leg. He is still recovering from the injury."

"And you believe it may be the same perpetrators?"

"I am convinced of it, possibly not the same marksman, no, he would be merely a hired assassin, but the man behind both crimes is surely the same," Bella said.

"But how do you reach this conclusion and who is this man?"

"Do you remember drawing an arrogant, foppish type of man with a high pointed collar outside the inn in village?"

"Yes, and you said you recognised him. Is that the man you believe culpable?"

Bella nodded. "Unfortunately, yes, my cousin, Granville Richmond."

The sound of voices in the hall announced the arrival of Captain Quentin and Dr. Grey into the drawing room.

After the introductions, Dr. Grey spoke, "A ball, probably from a musket, has grazed the top of Sir Jonathan's skull, but it is only a surface wound and should quickly heal. He also has a blow to the side of his cranium which is much more serious. He probably struck his head on a branch. That injury has sent him into a coma. If the blow was not too severe, he should recover consciousness within a few days. However, he will require expert care."

"Jackson has agreed to look after him, and Mr. Sanders will ensure a constant watch is kept over him should he come around," Captain Quentin said.

The news brought Catherine slight relief. The time the doctor had spent with his patient had been a very tense for her. She wanted to ask more about Sir Jonathan's health and state of well-being. Was he comfortable? But most of all, could she see him? But she knew that would be impossible.

"When he does wake up, undoubtedly, he will have a very bad headache, but he may also suffer loss of memory. We shall not know the extent until he regains consciousness," the surgeon said.

"It is getting late to journey back to Portsmouth, Dr. Grey, would you like to stay the night?"

"I thank you, Mrs. Quentin, the captain has already asked me to remain when I explained that the next few hours could be crucial."

Catherine's heart sank. Sir Jonathan's road to recovery was still plagued with danger. She bit her bottom lip and prayed silently for him.

* * * *

The next morning after breakfast, Admiral and Lady Mary arrived at Aston Grange. Although the admiral needed help descending from his carriage, he managed to hobble into the house. Catherine watched the arrivals from the upper landing where she had been hovering, trying to hear fresh news of Sir Jonathan from Dr. Grey.

"Got your note last night," the admiral said, "nearly came over then, but Lady Mary advised me otherwise. How is he?"

Captain Quentin stepped forward and invited his in-laws into the drawing room. A few moments later, Bella emerged from her room looking rather pale.

"Are you feeling unwell, Bella?" Catherine asked.

Bella smiled, as if she was very pleased about something. "No, a little out of sorts but I am perfectly well."

"The Admiral and Lady Mary have just arrived. They are in the library with Captain Quentin."

"Oh." Bella paused. "I had better go and greet them will you accompany me?"

Catherine shook her head. "I have a feeling they have come to discuss family matters, if so they will wish to be private. Besides, I'd like to write a letter to my mother. Is there any fresh news of Sir Jonathan?"

"Nothing new, he remains unconscious but Dr. Grey says his body is strong and we must pray for his recovery. But it might be unwise to mention too many details of the accident to your family. Your mother might decide it is too dangerous for you to remain in Hampshire and insist you return home. I wouldn't like to lose you, not for a few weeks."

"And I wouldn't want to leave, not now, not until Sir Jonathan has recovered," Catherine said.

"I understand." Bella nodded and descended the stairs.

Catherine watched her cross the great hall and enter the library, but instead of returning to her own room, she slipped along the corridor to Sir Jonathan's bed chamber. The door was slightly ajar, enabling her to hear the conversation from within.

"Sir Jonathan must be turned every two hours and his lips moistened with cooled, boiled water at five minute intervals," Dr. Grey said.

"Wouldn't a good tot of rum do the trick?"

"Do you want the man to choke?" the more cultured voice of the doctor replied.

"No sir, 'course not sir, only it always used to work on board ship."

"Aye, along with a good many other so-called cures. I've done my time as a navy surgeon Jackson, I know all the quack remedies."

Footsteps approaching from inside the sick room made Catherine jump back from the door. She walked towards her own room at the other end of the corridor. As she opened the door, she looked back and saw Dr. Grey descending the stairs and Captain Quentin's man, Jackson, accompanying him. There was no one else standing on the landing. She glanced along the corridor, Sir Jonathan's door stood wide open.

Dare she approach? Surely there would be a manservant in attendance. It was no time to dither. Either she went to look inside at the patient, or she returned to her own room. She slipped along to the entrance to his bed chamber and peered inside.

Sir Jonathan lay in the centre of the large tester bed, his dark wavy hair cascading onto his shoulders. Her heartbeat quickened at the sight of him immobile, she wanted to rush to his side and comfort him in some small way. Her senses aroused, pulse racing, she scanned the room, and took another tentative step inside. There didn't appear to be any other servants within. Sir Jonathan's head was bandaged, so he looked as though he was wearing a white nightcap, his nightshirt was open at the neck, exposing dark chest hair.

She swallowed deeply, her breathing became uneven, but not through fear of discovery. She felt an overwhelming desire to be near to him, each tentative step bringing her closer. She wanted to call out to him, but daren't in case anyone heard her. Silently, she mouthed his name, his given name, three times. His eyes were closed, but she was near enough to see the sweep of his dark lashes flutter. His eyelids flickered opened and he blinked.

She stepped back, covered her mouth with her hands to muffle her gasp. Again, his long eye lashes flicked open and he raised his hand slightly from the bed cover.

"Miss El..lis?" he groaned.

Panic tore through her—panic and joy. He was awakening but where were his attendants, the doctor, anyone but her? She turned and ran out of the room, reached the top of the stairs and shouted, "Sir Jonathan is calling he needs help!"

Sanders appeared at the bottom and Catherine repeated her cry. He raced up the steps two at a time and hurried into Sir Jonathan's room. This time Catherine waited outside on the landing at an appropriate distance. Dr. Grey, accompanied by Jackson, returned, went inside, and closed the door.

* * * *

The warm afternoon sun streamed in through Catherine's window. She didn't know how long she paced her room. She tried to read, to write her letter to her mother, to draw a few sketches but nothing worked, she couldn't concentrate on anything except to walk endlessly back and forth. She glanced out of the window several times, watched the birds feeding on the fruit in the walled garden, saw the occasional gardener digging potatoes, glanced over the parkland to the great trees in full foliage, all of these scenes might have at one time inspired her to draw, but not now. Part of her felt immense relief that he had gained his senses, if only for a short period. That he had recognised her was quite remarkable and even flattering. Could he possibly have some feelings for her?

It was more than she dared hope for because from the moment she had seen him stripped of his clothing and about to leap into a large barrel of soapy water she had fallen in love with Sir Jonathan Westwood. The exhilarating feelings coursing through her veins each time she thought of him, the nervous tension gripping her insides when she saw him, and the mental images haunting her dreams, drew her to one simple conclusion. She had experienced nothing similar with Rossi.

Rossi. She covered her face with her hands, how could she have been so foolish to believe herself in love with him?

Following a knock on her door, Martha entered. "Excuse me, miss, but Mrs. Quentin says will you join her and Lady Mary in the small parlour?"

Catherine smoothed down her muslin gown, checked her appearance in the glass, adjusted a few stray tendrils of hair, and attempted to settle her raging inner feelings. She took a deep breath and descended the stairs, but she couldn't resist a quick glance along the corridor at Sir Jonathan's room. The door was shut.

"Catherine, Lady Mary and I were taking tea and thought you might like to join us."

"Good afternoon, your ladyship," Catherine said, dropping the customary brief curtsy. "Tea would be most welcome, weak please and no milk."

Bella took another cup, opened her tea caddie, and sprinkled a small pinch of the precious leaves into the strainer. She locked the caddie before filling the cup with hot water from the urn. When the tea was at the preferred strength, she handed the cup to Catherine. "How is Sir Jonathan?"

"Dr. Grey says he has regained consciousness. Although, he has a bad headache, there does not appear to be any great loss of memory," Bella said, "Sanders tells me you raised the alarm."

Catherine hesitated before replying. She didn't want to explain to Bella what she was doing in a gentleman's bed chamber alone, but she didn't want to lie. "I was coming from my room," she said, "and I heard him calling out."

"Good that you took action when you did," Lady Mary said, "and thank heaven he is on the mend. Bella and I have been talking over a few matters. This shooting incident, I believe Bella has told you about the admiral and, well, we must all be very vigilant. We thought everything was over, and tranquillity had returned to Aston, but it seems we were mistaken. You must not go around the estate or village alone, and I don't count your maid. She must accompany you, but so must one of the menservants."

"But why should I be in danger?"

"Catherine, since the Peace there have been numerous highwaymen and ruffians roaming the countryside," Bella said. "There is one gang in particular working in this area of Hampshire. They target young women, usually servant girls, so you must look to your maid as well. Young women are being kidnapped; they are taken on ships, usually to France and thence to the Barbary coast of north Africa, where they command a high price when they are sold into harems."

"Goodness, I had no idea abduction was rife in the vicinity. This is all connected to the shooting of Sir Jonathan?" Catherine could hardly believe what she had heard. The most exciting occurrence in her own neighbourhood was usually the hue and cry after poachers or a servant girl running off to London. "Will this prevent the Earl and Countess coming to Penley?"

Lady Mary's expression looked dour. "I have written to my sister-in-law explaining the situation but for some reason she has her mind fixed on Penley. I don't think she ever liked me having the place. My brother was most kind and granted me a life-interest in the estate when I lost my dear Charles. The family are expected tomorrow and the ball has been fixed for the twenty-eighth of this month."

"In less than two weeks," Bella declared, "how can all the arrangements be made in so short a time?"

"Thankfully, that is Lady Norton's problem and not mine," Lady Mary replied.

* * * *

Jonathan's head throbbed. He stared up at the ceiling and tried to remember what he had collided with. He put his hand to the side of his head and felt the muslin bandage wrapped around. "What's this on my head?"

Dr. Grey stepped forward and explained who he was and what had happened. "I can give you some laudanum to dull the pain."

"I want none of your drugs," Jonathan said, "I might have cracked my head but I'll not have my wits nullified by your potions."

"A wise decision, Sir Jonathan," the doctor said, "however, you might find there are gaps in your memory, people you do not recognise, and you need rest. Your body has undergone a severe shock. How is your vision and hearing?"

Jonathan thought for a few moments, "My head feels stuffed with wool. My arms and legs are stiff. You say I was knocked unconscious, how am I supposed to feel?"

"I detect you do not make a good patient, sir, but I do advise a few days bed-rest."

"Bed-rest. I have never been confined to bed in my life."

Dr. Grey nodded. "Try it, sir, it works wonders with the ladies if you wish to drum up a bit of sympathy." He closed his bag. "My work is done, sir, should you need me again, Captain Quentin has my direction in Portsmouth. I bid you good-day sir."

Left alone, Jonathan closed his eyes. What had happened when he was riding with Ross? They were discussing matrimony and he was considering offering for Miss Ellis. Immediately her image flashed before him, but she was in his room, standing before him, at the end of his bed, calling his name as if willing him back to her world.

He had reached out to her, as if emerging from some dark abyss, and called to her but she had run away from him. His memory was playing tricks on him, imagining Miss Ellis coming to his rescue. Perhaps Dr. Grey was right, after all, he needed bed rest.

Tiredness welled up inside him. He closed his eyes but still he couldn't get the image of Miss Ellis standing at the foot of his bed out of his mind, until he drifted into an uneasy sleep.

Chapter Ten

An uneasy normality descended on Aston Grange over the next few days. Catherine kept busy with the watercolour portrait of Bella and helped Martha with her letters by writing simple sentences for the girl to read and copy. Overall, Martha made excellent progress, however, Catherine was mindful about keeping the girl occupied. On a few occasions, she had noticed her standing in the yard behind the kitchen talking to some of the younger menservants.

The watercolour of Bella was admired, not only by the subject, but also Captain Quentin and, much to Catherine's delight, Sir Jonathan. He kept to his bed chamber for two days after his accident. When he did emerge for dinner around six on the third evening, he was greeted warmly by the others, who were already seated in the dining room when he entered.

"Dashed glad to see you," Captain Quentin said as he rose from his seat, "why didn't you tell me, Bella, that Jonathan was joining us tonight?"

Bella looked bemused. "Because I didn't know, however, you are most welcome and I hope recovered."

He took his place, which Sanders and Jackson quickly laid for him, opposite Catherine. "I have caused enough trouble by lying abed, I have business to attend and precious little time left."

Catherine looked across the table at him, what did he mean? Would he be returning to London? She wanted to ask him but refrained, his movements should not be her concern, but the ache in her heart said otherwise.

"Are you planning to leave us?" Bella asked.

Inwardly Catherine thanked her hostess for asking the question she yearned to ask. Sir Jonathan acknowledged Bella's question, then looked at Captain Quentin as if there was some arrangement extant between them. "A particular matter requires my attention here, when it is settled I may have to go up to town to finalise some legal papers."

"Invitations arrived from Lord and Lady Norton today. The Penley ball is next Thursday week. Will you be joining our party?"

"If I may, Mrs. Quentin, I shall look forward to renewing my acquaintance with Norton. We were childhood friends. The family spent the summer at Penley, as we did here, but I've not seen him for...nearly twenty-five years."

"Were you acquainted with Lady Mary as a child?" Catherine asked.

"Indeed, Lady Mary used to organise our games, run circles around the Nortons' governess, and generally take command. I remember her being very protective of her brother and even offered to fight a duel on his behalf. She told him he had no business risking his life because he was the heir, it didn't seem to occur to her that ladies didn't fight duels either. But thinking on it, I recall she was highly skilled at fencing and could easily disarm us boys. Take my advice, Miss Ellis, do not cross swords with her ladyship."

"Thank you for the warning, Sir Jonathan, fortunately I have no intention of doing so. I shall stick to my paint brush and trust in my wits."

"Bravely said, Catherine," Bella said, "but have no fear of my stepmother. She is a loyal friend and delightful companion. I value her wisdom and often seek her advice. As to Lord and Lady Norton, our acquaintance is only slight. What I know of them comes solely from my stepmother."

About to ask after Lady Venetia, but not wishing to draw attention by doing so, Catherine hoped the lady may come up in conversation. She was eager to observe Sir Jonathan's reaction, but it was not to be.

Sanders and Jackson, followed by two menservants, brought in the food, placed all the dishes on the table, and began serving. It pleased Catherine that Sir Jonathan ate heartily—another indication of his recovery. However, she found her appetite had waned. She kept thinking about Lady Venetia. Would Sir Jonathan be taken with her, dance with her at the Penley ball and—she closed her mind to any further possibilities and pushed her meagre portion of food around her plate.

"Are you out of sorts?" Bella asked.

"Not in the slightest." Catherine smiled back at her hostess. "I usually walk more during the day and find our confinement restrictive."

"Miss Ellis, I have insisted that you and Bella remain in the house for your own good," Captain Quentin said, his tone authoritarian.

"Of course, you have," Bella intervened, "and both Miss Ellis and I understand, but there are only so many times one can take a turn around the garden without becoming giddy."

* * * *

After dinner, when the ladies had withdrawn, Ross offered his guest a glass of brandy.

"Just a small tot, please," Jonathan said, "Today my head has stopped throbbing, but I don't want to start it up again by getting foxed. What progress has been made to apprehend the villain who took a pot-shot at me?"

"I've sent out patrols to scout the area, made inquiries at the local inns along the turnpike road, and into Portsmouth, but turned up nothing." Ross took a large swig from his brandy glass.

"Whilst I was lying abed, I had plenty of time to think. We suspect Granville Richmond is behind this. We've had one sighting of him here in Aston and our own encounter with him in London. Where else has he been of late?"

"Jeremy has agents out following him, but from the last report, Richmond is very elusive and is known to use several aliases, especially with the new rich, anxious to make acquaintances amongst the *ton*.

Richmond has several identities and a few titles when the mood takes him to cut a sham."

"We've already decided the futility of trying to chase him all over London, and our plan was to lure him here. Have we not succeeded?"

Ross put his elbows on the table and hunched forwards. "He probably sent a paid lackey. We have no evidence to link him to the crime?"

"Then we must trap him, but first we need to find him. Miss Ellis drew a sketch of him, if we ask, could she not produce several drawings of him? We could help her by describing his features."

"And my men could take them around the inns and ale-houses where he is probably known by a different name. What a splendid idea. Shall I ask her, or would you rather speak to her?" Ross lifted a questioning eyebrow.

"I'll ask her," Jonathan said, but realised the swiftness of his reply and added, "I fell for that one, didn't I? Am I so transparent?"

Ross leaned back in his chair, "Would you like me to talk to Bella? Women are far better with these matters."

The notion appealed to Jonathan. "Could Mrs. Quentin find out if Miss Ellis might receive me favourably and impress upon her the urgency of my situation without telling her about my inheritance?"

Ross rolled his eyes, "Now that is a tall order."

* * * *

The following day, around noon, Lady Mary arrived at Aston Grange in her carriage. She had sent a note the previous evening inviting Bella and Miss Ellis to accompany her to Penley to call upon Lady Norton and her eldest daughter Lady Venetia. Catherine had mixed views about the call. Part of her wanted to see Lady Venetia but as long as the lady remained a figment of her imagination she could keep her at a distance. Once an introduction has been made, and if the lady was tolerable, then Sir Jonathan might—

No, she wanted to stay at Aston Grange, but how could she tell Bella? Perhaps she could use the excuse she was completing the drawings Sir Jonathan had asked her to do. Bella was most enthusiastic about the idea and encouraged her both before and after breakfast, pointing out her cousin's features and commenting on the length of his nose, hair style, and apparel in the finest detail. Once a master sketch was agreed upon, it was only a matter of reproducing several copies, something Catherine could manage effectively at speed. She put the sixth sketch into her portfolio and called Martha. Hiding at Aston Grange was not the answer. She would be turning down an opportunity to go out and form an opinion of a potential rival. Thus, Catherine joined the ladies and rode in the Richmond carriage, guarded by four armed outriders. Seated backwards, opposite Lady Mary and Bella, she did not glimpse the house until they were well inside the park and almost at the entrance.

As they descended, Catherine looked up at the Palladian frontage, the impressive carved stonework and the flowing stone staircase that swept up either side of the entrance to the main doors at first floor level. They mounted the stairs, entered a reception lobby, and were conducted through the grandest hall Catherine had ever seen. Large gilt-framed mirrors hung on both sides and light streamed in at the far end through huge sash windows which could be raised to the height of doors to enable air and people to circulate from the terrace beyond.

The butler led them to the drawing room, which overlooked the grounds and the lake beyond.

After they were announced, and Lady Mary made the customary introductions, the ladies were invited to sit. Catherine took a seat near to Bella, where she had a good view of Lady Venetia and her mother.

Physically, Lady Venetia was as her aunt had described her: the Norton red hair, a liberal sprinkling of freckles, small features, and a tall, slender figure. She wore a muslin gown trimmed with pale green ribbon and she smiled occasionally.

"How did you find London?" Lady Mary asked.

Lady Norton spoke, "Very tiresome, extremely crowded, and awash with soldiers and sailors. I know the Peace has brought many sons home to their families, but some officers are most awkward in a ballroom and have very little conversation."

"My husband, Captain Quentin, who is one of those *awkward* officers, would say he has little time for the trivia of polite society."

"I only speak as I find, but Mrs. Quentin, you have the advantage, your father is an admiral and you know the service. I'm sure you have entertained many naval officers at your father's table and have the skill to put your guests at ease."

Bella nodded. "And Penley, does the house please you?"

Lady Norton looked at her daughter and gave a condescending nod. Lady Venetia took her cue and began, "Mama and I have been drawing up a list of improvements we believe are necessary. Papa has a childhood love of the place, but alas, Mama and I cannot see it."

"Improvements?" Lady Mary echoed, "What sort of improvements?"

"There is a distinct lack of space for storage, especially for my best gowns," Lady Norton said.

"And mine, why I've had my maids fold and unfold and fold again. Some of my best gowns have had to remain in the trunks. I only hope my best coming-out gowns are not creased beyond wear."

"I am sure the maids will work hard to ensure you gown is pressed and looking as elegant as ever by the day of the ball. What colour will you be wearing Mary?" Lady Norton turned to her sister-in-law and tapped her forearm with her fan. Catherine could not resist a slight smile as Lady Mary strove to flick the fan away as if it was an undesirable insect.

"Hadn't really thought about it," Lady Mary replied, "I shall insist the admiral wears his full dress uniform, his man will bring him to the garden entrance; those stairs will be far too much for him."

"And how is dear Henry's leg?" Lady Norton asked.

"Mending nicely, "Lady Mary replied, "although he cannot walk great distances and if he has to stand he becomes very grumpy."

"I fear my stepmother deludes you, my father is never grumpy, he is downright cantankerous." Bella said and the other ladies burst into giggles. "Lady Venetia, did you enjoy your first Season?"

"Most of it," she replied, "the balls were splendid affairs but some were nothing more than a crush. Why I can remember promising dances to partners who when the dance came around, couldn't get through the throng to claim me. But there were always others to fill the vacant places."

Lady Norton smiled. "Of course, Venetia was extremely popular, however, several of the offers she received proved quite unsuitable and I don't think you wanted to marry any of them, did you?"

"Most certainly not, but if I had received an offer from a duke or marquis, I might have been tempted to hear him out, but I suspect I shall have to settle for an earl."

Catherine raised her eyebrows, Lady Venetia was proud, but would she accept Sir Jonathan's rank, if he offered for her? Would she have her head turned by his handsome face perhaps at the ball? The mere thought of him proposing to Lady Venetia was almost more than she could bear. A sharp pain stabbed her chest and she struggled silently, fighting to control her emotions by taking long, slow breaths. *Lady Venetia is young, just seventeen. But not too young to get married.*

* * * *

By the following morning, Catherine had completed another six drawings of the man she now knew was Bella's cousin, Mr. Granville Richmond. Although her first sketch had been more in the style of a satirical caricature, the new portraits in coloured pastels were small enough to carry in the pocket of a top coat and life-like enough, according to Bella, to identify the man.

"Why does Sir Jonathan want so many similar portraits," Catherine asked Bella as they sat in the small parlour after breakfast.

"He is trying to locate Granville and Ross is assisting him. It is estate business concerning the rightful ownership of Aston Grange."

Catherine said, "I have the greatest sympathy for Sir Jonathan—to return home because of the loss of his mother and brother, only to find his father gone and his business affairs in shreds. It must be very disconcerting to have one's home taken away and those you hold most dear, lost forever. And if those factors were not sufficient burden to carry, his life is threatened."

"I do believe you have developed a *tendre* for Sir Jonathan, am I correct?"

Heat flared in Catherine's cheeks. "I don't know what you are talking...oh, I suppose I have." She let out a long sigh. At last she could confess to someone.

"And you don't know what to do about it?"

"How did you guess?"

"Oh, Catherine, do not forget I fell in love myself only a few months ago when Captain Quentin came into the county, and although we should have been a perfect match, when does the course of true love ever run smoothly? Ross proposed to me the morning after the Summer Ball at Penley, foolishly, I turned him down. No sooner had I uttered the words, than I regretted them. But I'd bruised his ego, and men generally need some encouragement."

"Whatever do you mean?"

"I have the notion that Sir Jonathan thinks very highly of you, and you never know what a few dances can do to a man."

Their conversation was interrupted by a knock on the door and the butler entered. "Mr. and Mrs. Winters are in the hall. They wish to speak to you and Miss Ellis. They say it is very urgent."

"Oh, dear, I do hope my uncle does not bear bad news from home," Catherine said.

"We had better find out. Sanders, please show them in."

Her aunt couldn't wait to be formally announced. She rushed across the room, took Catherine's hand, and patted it as if to impart some terrible woe.

"Good morning, Mr. Winters," Bella said, "Won't you and your wife be seated?"

"Of course, most kind, Mrs. Quentin." he glared at his wife, who was still comforting Catherine. "Mrs. Winters, stop clucking like a mother hen and sit down."

Aunt Winters turned around to face him. "Of course, Mr. Winters, excuse me Mrs. Quentin."

Catherine let out a silent sigh of relief, but was anxious to know what had distressed her aunt. However, she was surprised by Mr. Winters' terse tone.

"What brings you both to Aston Grange this morning so urgently," Bella asked.

"A letter has arrived from Mr. Ellis," Aunt. Winters said, with tension in her voice and a worried expression on her face.

Mr. Winters pressed his fingers together. "It appears my brother-in-law does not approve of his daughter painting whilst she is staying in Hampshire. He gave no reason for his aversion to what appears, in my view, to be an exceedingly good pastime for a lady. However, upon receipt of your letter, Catherine, requesting your oils, easel, and spare canvases to be sent to the parsonage, Mr. Ellis has decided you are to go home and he and my sister are coming to fetch you."

"I do not know what to say, Mrs. Quentin, I went all a-flutter when Mr. Winters gave me the intelligence. What are we to do? I asked him, has our behaviour or care been wanting? I only allowed

Catherine to stay with you because I thought she would benefit from your company and now I feel I have done something dreadful." She took a handkerchief from her cuff and dabbed her eyes.

Bella turned to Catherine. "Do you know why your father should have acted in this manner?"

Catherine didn't know what to say, or how much to tell them. She trusted Bella, and she should have been able to trust her aunt and uncle, they were her family, but would knowledge of her behaviour colour their opinion of her? "Can I have your assurances that what I have to say will not be repeated elsewhere to anyone?"

Mr. Winters replied with a stony expression. "I do hope this isn't going to ruin reputations."

"Oh, my goodness, Catherine, has something happened to you whilst you have been with us?" Mrs. Winters cried.

"No," Catherine assured them. "I have spent nearly two weeks in Hampshire and passed my time most comfortably at the parsonage and here, thanks to Mrs. Quentin. About six months ago, my father engaged an art master from Manchester to instruct me. His name was Mr. Rossi."

"Rossi? I don't recall anyone of that name," Mr. Winters said.

Catherine took a deep breath and related the story to them. "He couldn't marry me because he already had a wife and children in London."

"Oh, my goodness, what infamy," Mrs. Winters cried, "you could have been guilty of bigamy."

"I tried to explain to my father that Rossi had tempted me to marriage because he had offered me a life as a professional artist, painting portraits in his studio, but my father did not consider such occupation appropriate for a lady. Papa might think Rossi has followed me and sending for my artist's materials has confirmed his suspicion. I regret if I have caused you any anxiety, dear aunt and uncle, because you have both showed me nothing but kindness and consideration whilst I have been with you. I shall tell my parents so, when they arrive, but my father can be a very stubborn man once he has an idea fixed in his mind."

"Mr. and Mrs. Winters," Bella said, "please accept my apology. It was only when I saw Catherine's sketches and recognised her talent, the idea of having my portrait painted occurred to me. And when she said she could work in oils, I was delighted. The pastel portrait she has completed is exquisitely executed. I was greatly looking forward to a larger painting in oils. Do you think if we approached Mr. Ellis, he might change his mind and allow Catherine to remain with us?"

Mr. Winters shook his head. "We can try, Mrs. Quentin, as Catherine says, my brother-in-law can be a very awkward man. However, I am looking forward to seeing my elder sister, again. She is an intelligent woman, highly accomplished, something of a blue-stocking in her youth, and an excellent conversationalist."

"When are my parents due?"

Mr. Winters scratched his head. "They plan to leave today which is Friday. I am assuming they will not travel on Sunday, so I will be surprised to see them before Tuesday. Yes, upon my reckoning, they'll be with us on Tuesday night or Wednesday around noon."

"Then I must make haste and prepare," Mrs. Winters said, "and we are going to the Penley Ball on Thursday. I shall have to have a word with Lady Norton on Sunday after service and ensure the Ellises are included in the parsonage invitation."

* * * *

It was the middle of the afternoon when Mr. and Mrs. Winters departed Aston Grange. The arrangement had been made for Bella to return Catherine to the parsonage on Monday, ready to welcome her parents. With only a few days to complete the water colour portrait of Bella and to sketch a few more pastels of Mr. Granville Richmond, Catherine set to work as soon as her aunt and uncle left.

She wanted to view the painting in differing light, it had only been a working piece, intended to explore the skin tones, textures and lighting she could use to effect when she started the oil painting. Now, there was a strong possibility she would be going home and would not be able to paint Bella from life. If her father did insist on returning home immediately, she decided she would paint Bella in oils at home, although with only sketches to use as reference it may not be her best work. That disappointed her, because she wanted to capture Bella's lively expression, her fine eyes and friendly disposition. Also, returning to Lancashire probably meant she would never see Sir Jonathan again. That prospect hung heavily over her.

Working alone in the library, at the far end where the light was good, she heard the door open and assumed it was one of the menservants. She looked up over her drawing board, her eyes widening, heart pounding as Sir Jonathan strode across the room towards her.

"Forgive me for disturbing you, Miss Ellis, I thought Mrs. Quentin would be with you, otherwise I..." he scanned the room, "I shouldn't be here alone with you."

Despite her temperature rising at the sight of him, she managed to speak, "If you are looking for Mrs. Quentin, I'm afraid she felt tired and has gone to her chamber to rest, can I help you?"

"Actually, I wanted to thank you for the sketches. The likeness is remarkable and to have completed so many in the short time available."

"You flatter me, sir, I have only seen the gentleman once and then at a distance, I could not have drawn him without considerable input from Captain and Mrs. Quentin."

Sir Jonathan smiled. "Your modesty does you credit, Miss Ellis."

"Thank you," she said and continued to work as he walked around the library, but her concentration had been disturbed. She stood back from her drawing board acutely aware of his presence. She looked up at him, standing only a few feet away. His wavy hair tied back and his dark features gave him a broody expression. He folded his arms and stood poised, as if there was something he wanted to say.

"Will you be attending the ball at Penley?" he asked.

"I hope so, but it is not certain. My parents are coming to Hampshire to take me home. They are expected at the parsonage on Tuesday. Doubtless my uncle and aunt will try to persuade them to stay a few days, but my father can be a very determined man. If he decides to leave before the ball, then I shall have to go with them."

His brow creased. "But I thought you planned to stay at least six weeks."

"That was the original plan and I am most disappointed I can remain no longer. However, I would like to go to the ball, if only to say my farewells to everyone who has been most kind to me whilst I have been in Hampshire."

"And your father is expected on Tuesday?"

"Uncle Winters believes so, he has calculated the journey most precisely, and anticipated that my parents would not travel on Sunday. As to that I cannot answer for my father, he is a most practical man and does not believe in wasting time."

"And yet he is prepared to travel several days from the north on your behalf. He must hold you very dearly."

"Yes, I am convinced he does." She didn't want to say any more because she didn't want Sir Jonathan to know about Rossi, or why her father had left Lancashire in haste. If only Sir Jonathan had been the one to propose to her instead of an art master who was already wed.

The door flew open and Captain Quentin strode in. He halted abruptly after a few paces. "Ah, Jonathan, Miss Ellis...er...I hope I am not interrupting you?"

"No," they both replied in unison. Captain Quentin smiled and rubbed his jaw.

"I came to thank Miss Ellis for the sketches she has done of Richmond," Jonathan said.

"Indeed, Miss Ellis, they have been most useful, please accept my thanks too. Bella tells me you will be leaving us on Monday, I shall miss your company and I know my wife will particularly. Did you know Jonathan that Mr. and Mrs. Ellis are expected at the parsonage next week?"

"Yes," he replied, "Miss Ellis has told me."

"Er...could I have a word with you Jonathan, in private, perhaps we could go to the study?"

* * * *

Jonathan followed Ross into the study, a small room at the back of the house where most of the estate records were kept. He glanced around at the room, which had changed little since his boyhood. He waited for Ross to offer him a seat.

"I feel awkward," Ross said, "asking you to sit down in your own house."

"The Grange isn't mine. Even if my father hadn't been cheated out of it, you hold the tenancy until Lady Day. Legally this is your house."

"Is it too early for a drink?" Ross asked.

"I'm sure the sun is over the yardarm in some part of the world," Jonathan said, "a shot of rum wouldn't go amiss."

Ross took a dark bottle out of a cupboard along with two small glasses and filled both. He handed one to Jonathan. "You might need this. Richmond has been sighted in Portsmouth."

Anger surged through Jonathan's veins. He took the rum and downed it in one swallow. "When?"

"Two days ago, he was doing business with a merchantman but he wasn't calling himself Richmond. Thanks to Miss Ellis's sketches, an inn keeper identified him as the Count of Alonso, would you believe?"

"It explains why Jeremy's agents haven't tracked him in London. What's the plan? My first reaction is to ride to Pompey, flush the rat out, and despatch him."

"Sit down, my friend," Ross said, "we both have good reason to see Richmond brought to book, but murder is a crime in the eyes of the law regardless of what the victim has done. Another?"

Jonathan held out his glass for a refill. "His presence in the area puts him squarely behind the attempt on my life."

"Only circumstantial, as always Richmond uses lackeys to do his dirty work. I have men posted around the docks, checking his movements. It's not just Richmond I'm after, I want to smash his band of pirates and their despicable trade once and for all, we must be ready to move at a moment's notice." Ross poured them both another drink.

"Most commendable captain, to victory." He raised his glass in salute and drank the contents.

When he had finished his, Ross said, "Now what progress with Miss Ellis? I didn't interrupt anything in the library, did I?"

"My mind is set. I understand Mr. Ellis is coming to the parsonage on Tuesday. I do not know what brings him south so urgently, but it can only be to my advantage. I shall seek an interview with him and ask for his permission to propose to his daughter."

"My, that will set the neighbourhood a-flutter, a marriage proposal and a ball all in one week."

Chapter Eleven

The following Sunday, Catherine sat in the Aston Grange pew with Bella, the captain and Sir Jonathan, although the Quentins were between them, she felt exhilarated just to be close to him. Occasionally, she thought she caught him looking along the row in her direction, or perhaps he was bored with waiting for the service to begin.

"When is the parson going to get started?" Admiral Richmond complained to his wife from the pew behind.

"Hush, we await the party from Penley," Lady Mary said.

"Then your brother should do better with his time-keeping. We're all waiting here like geese stuffed for the oven."

Catherine couldn't help but smile at the admiral's remark and shifted in her seat. She wouldn't have said anything but it was rather impolite of the Penley party to be late. Would Lady Venetia would be with them and how would Sir Jonathan react to meeting her? A slight twinge of jealousy began to fester inside her as she waited. Muffled noises, coughing and the occasional sneeze broke the uneasy silence.

The sound of a man clearing his throat made her glance over her shoulder. Admiral Richmond leaned forward towards his son-in-law, "I've had enough of this infernal waiting, tell Winters to get on with the service. I don't see why we should wait another minute for Norton."

Captain Quentin turned and said, "The parson is only doing his duty—"

"Duty. Confound the man. He needs to be reminded which side of his bread's buttered. You're the legal tenant of the Grange and thus Winters' living, instruct him to begin before my legs get so stiff I'll need to be strapped to a gate to get me home."

"Henry, please remember you're in God's house," Lady Mary whispered.

"Perhaps you should remind your brother next time you see him that when he lives in a country parish it is his duty to show his face at Sunday service."

Captain Quentin stood up, "Excuse me," he said.

The captain strode down the aisle to the back of the church where Mr. Winters stood. Catherine was too far away to hear what he said, despite the silence that befell the congregation. Within a few moments, the organ struck up, bringing everyone to their feet.

Mr. Winters' sermon droned on. Catherine did not listen to a word; instead she used the time for reflection. Somehow she had to convince her father that her desire to paint was entirely her own. Rossi had gone and she had had no further contact with him, nor did she want to see him again. The man had deceived her. Only now, with her feelings for Sir Jonathan so strong, did she realise she had never been in love with Rossi. Foolishly, she had allowed his flattery to influence her. Perhaps if she explained to her father, he might understand and allow her to remain a few more weeks in Hampshire. She leaned forwards and said a few silent prayers based on her hopes, and then glanced along the pew. Her eyes locked with Sir Jonathan's.

* * * *

Jonathan, accompanied by Ross, followed the Admiral and Lady Mary out of the church. Mr. Winters paid his respects to them in the porch. "How is the leg today, sir?"

"Not helped by sitting in your church for an inordinate length of time, sir," the admiral said, "I only hope St. Peter is more mindful of his flock and doesn't keep faithful souls waiting."

"Indeed sir, but with Lord Norton newly arrived, I'm sure you understand I delayed the service only out of respect for his rank in the parish."

"Bah! Don't give me your excuses sir, I'll have none of it and if my agent secures your living next month at the auction, you'll dance to my tune, Mr. Winters."

"Very well, sir." He bowed to the admiral, who was hurried away by his wife.

Jonathan shook the parson's hand. "Mr. Winters, I understand Mr. Ellis will be with you from Tuesday. There is a matter I wish to discuss with him, would you be so kind as to send word when he arrives?"

"Most certainly," Mr. Winters said, still shaking Jonathan's hand, "as soon as he crosses my threshold I will send my stable boy."

Jonathan wondered whether he should take the parson into his confidence, after all he might need an ally in dealing with Mr. Ellis. Then he saw Mrs. Winters hurrying along the path to greet Lady Mary and thought better of trusting the parson. He stepped aside to allow Mr. Winters to greet the Quentins and saw Miss Ellis waiting behind him.

She was framed in the church doorway, looking very pretty in a white muslin gown with a crimson spencer and matching bonnet. Her dark mahogany curls gathered at either side of her face. They had travelled together in the Quentin's carriage, but he had been sitting opposite Mrs. Quentin and had only been able to steal occasional glances at Miss Ellis, as he had done in the church. The more he thought of her, the more convinced he became of the advantages matrimony could bring him. Could he convince her father to part with her? More importantly, could he convince her he would make an ideal husband?

"Well, my friend, aren't you going to say your farewells?" Ross slapped him on the shoulder.

"Farewells? What do you mean? To whom?"

"To Miss Ellis, of course."

"But...I thought she wasn't leaving until Tuesday?" Jonathan looked anxiously between husband and wife.

"Oh, dear Bella, didn't you mention it? Sadly, Miss Ellis returns to the parsonage today to await her parents."

The news hit Jonathan hard, but he hoped it didn't show in his face. "I thought she was leaving on Tuesday?"

"Yes that was the arrangement," Mrs. Quentin replied, "but as we were coming into the village today, it seems opportune for her to remain at the parsonage rather than make a special journey on Tuesday. I thought Ross would have told you."

"Then, if you will excuse me, I must pay my respects for all the work she has done to help us." Aware of his hand shaking, Jonathan pushed the offending limb behind his back. He tensed, as if he was waiting for the first shot to find its mark at the beginning of a sea skirmish. The Quentins walked towards the Richmonds, leaving Jonathan to speak to Miss Ellis, who had been talking to her uncle.

She spoke first, "Did you enjoy singing the hymns, Sir Jonathan?"

"Yes, Miss Ellis, hymns have a satisfying familiarity about them and gladden the heart. However, I particularly enjoyed singing to your accompaniment when I stayed at the parsonage."

"Sir Jonathan, you are flattering me, I know the limits of my ability at the pianoforte, however, it was a pleasure to accompany you and I hope I shall have the opportunity to do so again."

"And I hope you remain in the neighbourhood for a few days more. It would be a pity if you missed the ball. I do not want to be too forward, but I hoped you would reserve me a set or two?"

He admired the sparkle in her eyes. Did she look at everyone in this way, or was her gaze for him alone? Could he hope?

* * * *

Jonathan received a note from Mr. Winters on Wednesday morning. The stable boy who had brought it asked if there was a reply. The boy was devouring a tankard of small ale and a generous wedge of buttered bread when Jonathan found him in the kitchen.

"Don't think they know how to feed boys at the parsonage, sir," Jackson said. "You should join the navy lad, when we gets to fight the Frenchies again. You get good victuals on board ship."

Jonathan looked at the boy, a scrawny lad not more than ten years old. "Take this note straight back to Mr. Winters, and no tarrying along the way, boy. I shall be calling at the parsonage at noon. I don't want to arrive before I'm expected. Here's a coin to make sure you get there before me." He flipped the lad a halfpenny for his trouble.

The lad's eyes lit up as he caught the coin. "Thank you sir, I'll be as quick as I can."

"I've never seen a skinny bag of bones move so fast," Jackson laughed. "Shall I send word around to the stables, sir? Would you be wanting the carriage or a horse?"

"Horseback will serve my purpose." He turned to leave.

"Excuse me, Sir Jonathan, but the captain says we have to guard you at all times. Let me or a couple of the others come as escort."

"Agreed, Jackson, meet me in the stable yard three-quarters of an hour before noon." Jonathan made his way upstairs to his bed chamber, selected his best boots, and called for one of the menservants to help him put them on. He took a deep breath, glanced in the mirror, and pulled down the front of his coat. He picked up his hat, gloves and riding crop and made his way downstairs.

"Jackson told me you were riding to the parsonage," Ross called from the great hall, "do you mind if I ride with you, only as far as the village, I'll leave the parsonage to you. I hope you find Mr. Ellis amenable."

Jonathan raised his hand in salute, waited for Ross and together they strode through the kitchen towards the stable yard.

Soon, they were on their way to the village with Jackson and McCoy accompanying them. They covered the distance at a slow trot and arrived in good time. They dismounted at the church and walked their mounts along High Street.

"I've spoken to Bella and she believes you and Miss Ellis would be a splendid match. Also, she is convinced the young lady is quite taken with you. Be encouraged Jonathan, a man needs confidence when he's about to propose. Get her father on your side, and the rest should be plain sailing."

"Is that how you won Mrs. Quentin?"

"Ah, it wasn't that easy. I was fortunate the admiral gave me his full support, but wisely left the final decision to his daughter. I wish you well. When you're out of doors, keep Jackson at your side. Remember we can't be too vigilant. When you've finished, meet me at the inn, whatever the outcome. Finally, good luck, Jonathan. Mr. Ellis is a numbskull if he turns you down."

* * * *

A female servant answered the door at the parsonage but Mr. Winters must have been watching out for his caller because he appeared in the hall almost as soon as Jonathan had crossed the threshold.

"Sir Jonathan, I received your note and welcome, perhaps you would like to step into my book room?" Mr. Winters held open the door.

Although Jonathan had stayed a night at the parsonage he had not been inside the small room at the front of the house where Mr. Winters composed his sermons. The walls were lined with books, several volumes were stacked high on the large table which served as a desk along with writing materials.

"Thank you for informing me so promptly about Mr. Ellis' arrival, would it be possible for you to introduce me to the gentleman as there is a matter I wish to discuss with him?"

"Of course, Sir Jonathan, it would be a pleasure. I have already explained to my brother-in-law your wishes, but he was quite baffled as to the nature of any business he might have with you. He can be very blunt, Sir Jonathan, a typical Lancashire man, a character trait often found in persons from that part of the country, I am given to understand by my sister. However, you wouldn't care perhaps to confide in me first, so I can smooth the path, so to speak, would you?"

Jonathan cleared his throat. "With the greatest respect for your profession, Mr. Winters, it would be preferable if I spoke to Mr. Ellis alone. Could I trouble you to introduce me to the gentleman and then leave us?"

Mr. Winters' face dropped. Jonathan had come to see Mr. Ellis and employing an intermediary would not augur well.

"As you wish." Mr. Winters gave the bell-pull a tug and the same servant who had opened the door before, entered the room. "Ask Mr. Ellis if he would kindly step into my book room."

"Yes, sir, at once sir." the woman dropped a short curtsey and left the room.

When Mr. Ellis entered, he was not in the least how Jonathan had imagined him. Miss Ellis's father was a short man of rotund proportions, white hair, white whiskers, and red cheeks.. What does Mrs. Ellis look like? Miss Catherine Ellis certainly did not take her looks from her father.

Mr. Winters made the customary introductions and then hovered. Jonathan glared at him for several moments before the parson made a feeble excuse to withdraw. When the door closed behind his brother-in-law, Mr. Ellis looked up at Jonathan and said, "Sir Jonathan, what is so private and important to demand my urgent attention?"

"Sir, I had but been a few days in the neighbourhood, when Miss Ellis came to my attention. She appeared a very calm and capable young lady for her years, accomplished and frugal, in short sir, the very sort of young lady that I am looking for in a wife. I would like to ask your permission to approach Miss Ellis with a proposal of marriage."

"And your circumstances sir, what are they?"

"I am from a long and distinguished line of country gentlemen, I have not long come into the title, which as a second son, I did not expect to inherit. I have served for over twenty years in His Majesty's Britannic Navy and rose to the rank of Post Captain. I have prize money of ten thousand pounds. However, I have resigned my commission and intend to manage my estates."

"All very well sir. What of your real position? Your debt?"

Jonathan gulped, the man's blunt question struck at his core. "There are two estates. My ancestral home, Westwood in the county of Worcestershire, is mortgaged for fifteen thousand pounds. I am applying to the King's Bench to dispute ownership of the second estate Aston Grange in this parish."

As Mr. Ellis raised his bushy white eyebrows, his forehead creased. "So, you have ten thousand but want fifteen. Is it your intention to ask me to make up the difference and more with my daughter's dowry?"

"No sir, it is not. I would take Miss Ellis without a penny, if she would marry me before Michaelmas." Jonathan felt Mr. Ellis' gaze range over him, as if weighing him up.

"How sir? Explain," Mr. Ellis demanded.

"I stand to inherit five thousand from my mother's marriage settlement on my wedding day. The bank will foreclose on September twenty-eighth. I intend to settle. I have the prospect of further monies when the Prize Court has determined my portion. I do not pretend to be wealthy, Miss Ellis will have to live frugally and manage her household accordingly. It may be many years before legal ownership of Aston Grange is decided, but I will fight to recover what is rightfully mine."

"Then why aren't you marrying for money, surely there's plenty of rich gentlemen wanting a title for their daughter?"

"That would be dishonourable. I have made my own way and money fighting at sea. When my brother and father died, I did expect to inherit my family seat, estates, and wealth, but that is not to be. I am not here to deceive you, sir, but merely to ask for your daughter. I believe I could make her happy and that she would be a great comfort to me." Jonathan looked into Mr. Ellis's stony face, hoping for some indication of consent. He saw none.

"Have you spoken to Catherine yet?"

"No, sir, I have not and would not do so until I had your permission."

"And what if I hadn't come south?"

"I would have journeyed north to see you."

"And what if I offered you five thousand *not* to marry my daughter, would you take it, sir, and leave my daughter alone?"

"Mr. Ellis, if this is some sort of test of my integrity, I find it crass. I do not want your money, but I do want to marry your daughter. I have approached you in an honourable manner. I have made no secret of my circumstances and am prepared to engage upon further discussion with your lawyers, if required. I wish to propose to Miss Ellis and marry her before Michaelmas."

Mr. Ellis remained silent. He took a few paces across the room, turned, and retraced his steps. "Catherine has persuaded us to stay a few days, she wishes to attend a ball tomorrow; I suppose you will also be in attendance?"

Jonathan nodded. "Lord and Lady Norton have come to Penley for the remainder of the summer."

"I'm sure Catherine will enjoy the ball, she likes music and dancing, I would not wish to spoil her evening." He turned and looked directly at Jonathan, "I did not intend to throw aspersion on your integrity, sir, I act merely as a protective father. You have my permission to address my daughter. Might I suggest after the ball? Whether she accepts you will be her decision. I hope she does and here is my hand upon it."

* * * *

As Mr. Winters' small carriage turned into the gates of Penley Court, Catherine breathed a sigh of relief their journey was nearly done. She squashed between her aunt and mother, whilst her uncle and father sat opposite. The Ellises' had come post chaise south and, therefore, did not have a vehicle at their disposal.

Mr. Ellis wore a dour expression. "This is a rough road, Winters. Norton should repair his driveway if he expects a large crowd, gives the visitor a bad impression before he's got a leg in the door."

"Indeed, brother, I cannot agree more." The carriage slowed and lurched to the side. "There seems to be an inordinate number of ruts in the road tonight. I do hope our return journey is less bumpy."

"How can that be," Mr. Ellis growled. "We are coming back the same way, aren't we?"

Mr. Winters nodded, dipped his head, and covered his mouth with his hand.

"Penley has a well-proportioned ballroom, doesn't it, Catherine? And I am sure there will be plenty of young men wanting to dance with you." Aunt Winters said.

"I have only visited Penley once," Catherine reminded her aunt, "and in your company. I assume the large hall will be used as the ballroom and with the windows raised there will be access to the terrace and conservatory at the rear."

"Quite right, my dear, the place is perfect for entertaining on a grand scale. As I keep telling your mother, we are most fortunate to have the acquaintance of the three most prominent families in the neighbourhood and several others in the adjacent parishes. I suspect there will be a good turn-out tonight. Of course, when Lady Mary held her summer ball in June, there was the most awful crush—why, there was scare room for couples to make up the sets. But it was so engaging to see so many faces from all over the county."

Eventually, the carriage halted. They descended and entered the house. As they queued to be announced, Catherine stood on tip-toe. She wanted to scan the heads, searching for one in particular.

"Who are you looking for?" her mother asked.

"The Quentin party," she replied, the heat of a blush sweeping her neck and face.

"Do not worry, they won't be far off, and you look very well in your new gown, I'm sure you will not be short of partners."

"Do you think so, Mama?" Catherine said but her heart sank at the sight of so many ladies dressed in silks and satins with bright jewels sparkling from intricate hairstyles. Several diamond necklaces were also being worn. She stretched to her full height, but couldn't see Sir Jonathan's dark wavy hair or his companions, the Quentins.

Eventually, they were announced and greeted by their host and hostess. Catherine was surprised that Lady Venetia wasn't with them, but she didn't dare ask about the young lady's whereabouts. Mr. Winters explained his connection to the Ellis' to his lordship, and they moved into the ballroom. People stood in their parties talking as the dancing wasn't yet underway. Catherine's heart skipped a beat as Sir Jonathan, in his dark naval uniform, approached their party. He carried the gold epaulettes of post-captain rank proudly on his broad shoulders. His white linen contrasted with his dark wavy hair, tied back with black ribbon. But when he smiled at her, joy surged through her. She could no longer deny her strong feelings for him. It had been the previous Sunday since she had seen him at church, although he had called at the parsonage. His call had been business, not social, in nature, so the ladies had not been privileged to his company.

He made formal acknowledgement of Mr. and Mrs. Winters, Mr. Ellis, and paused to be introduced to Mrs. Ellis. The formalities over, he turned to Catherine. "Good evening, Miss Ellis." He lifted her gloved hand to his lips. She gazed up at him, lost in his dark eyes. "I hope you will grant me the pleasure of the supper dance?"

"Of course, Sir Jonathan." Were his eyes sparkling for her alone? It was too much to hope for, but her heart fluttered in anticipation of a wonderful evening. "Where are Captain and Mrs. Quentin?"

"They are with Admiral Richmond and Lady Mary. Unfortunately, the admiral's leg is causing him trouble and he needed to sit. I think you will find them in the small salon to the right." He indicated the way without taking his eyes off hers.

The first chords of music struck up and people began to move to the edges of the room. "The dancing is about begin. Perhaps we had better go and pay our respects to the Richmonds and the Quentins," she said and blinked, he was still holding her gloved fingertips.

"If you will excuse me, until later," he said, letting go of her hand and after a brief nod to her party, he turned and strode across the dance floor.

"He's very dashing in his uniform," Mrs. Ellis said, "and I would love to stay and watch the dancing but I think your father would prefer a seat. Shall we go into another room?"

They followed Mr. and Mrs. Winters into a small salon where Admiral Richmond was seated with two elderly gentlemen. Mr. Winters approached them and introduced Mr. Ellis. Following the usual formalities, the admiral pointed to a couple of vacant chairs and Mr. Ellis and Mr. Winters sat down.

Lady Mary and Mrs. Quentin approached the ladies. This time it was Catherine's turn to introduce her mother.

"The dancing has just started; wouldn't you like to see the couples?" Bella asked and nudged Catherine's elbow.

"Why yes, what else is there to see at a ball?" Catherine replied.

"Run along then you two, whilst we more senior ladies complain about our gentlemen abandoning us." Lady Mary chuckled. "I sometimes wonder why gentlemen past the flush of youth ever bother to attend balls at all."

"Isn't their purpose the same as ours," Mrs. Ellis said, "to see and be seen, to observe every minute change in our neighbours, and to talk about them afterwards?"

"Mrs. Ellis, I believe you are a woman after my own heart, except I find to see my neighbours these days I am reliant on my lorgnettes." Lady Mary glanced at Catherine and Bella, "Off you go then, and see if you can find out where my son-in-law has disappeared to."

Catherine followed Bella, who edged her way into the ballroom and found a place at the far end, close to the terrace. With the windows fully raised a cool breeze floated into the ballroom.

"The air is so much fresher here," Bella said. "Can you see my husband?"

Catherine stretched on tip-toe but she couldn't see the captain. "No, but look who Sir Jonathan is dancing with." A sharp stab pricked Catherine's heart as she gazed at the couple moving up the set towards them.

"Oh, dear," Bella sighed. "I suppose we should have expected that."

Sir Jonathan's attention was fixed firmly upon his partner. Catherine's heart felt heavy, as she clung to every movement of the dancing couple. Lady Venetia danced with the elegance of a swan. Her pure white silk gown moulded to her slender form as she glided gracefully within her set. She had a long neck and held her head high. Her auburn tresses had been tamed with small ribbon bows each containing a sparkling diamond. And even her freckled face seemed to have been covered or treated with some cream or potion, because her complexion appeared remarkable fine and clear.

"We can come away, if you prefer? I'm sure we can occupy ourselves more usefully than gawp at that lady. Has Sir Jonathan asked you to dance yet?" Bella whispered.

"I've promised him the supper dance, but eating couldn't be further from my mind at present."

"If he asked for the supper dance, then you have nothing to worry about. He probably felt obliged to open the dancing with the host's daughter out of politeness. I doubt if there is any attraction between the two of them."

Catherine wished she could feel the same as Bella. "Take a look around the room. The gossips will have them engaged before the end of the evening. I'm beginning to wish I had stayed at the parsonage."

"Nonsense, the night is still young, who knows what might happen," Bella said.

At that moment, a lieutenant in full dress uniform, approached and bowed. "Mrs. Quentin, how pleasant to see you looking so fine. Would you be so kind as to introduce me to your friend?"

"Of course, Lieutenant Collins." Bella turned to Catherine and made the necessary introduction, explaining that Catherine and her parents were staying at the parsonage with Mr. and Mrs. Winters. "Lieutenant Collins has the command of my father's sloop, the *Vesta*. She is decommissioned, but the admiral likes to keep her sea-ready in Portsmouth with a skeleton crew aboard." She turned back to the officer. "How are you?"

"I am very well, Mrs. Quentin, and delighted to see you and Captain Quentin again."

Bella looked around. "Have you seen him? I appear to have lost him."

Lieutenant Collins smiled. "I doubt if that is likely, Mrs. Quentin, however, I did see him in the reception area only a few minutes ago when I arrived. Too late, I'm afraid, to be introduced to Lord Norton. However, not too late to meet you, Miss Ellis, would you care to dance?"

Catherine looked quickly at Bella, who nodded slightly. "Thank you Lieutenant Collins, I believe the next set will be forming in a few moments." The music stopped and Catherine watched Sir Jonathan escort Lady Venetia from the ballroom, hoping he might glance back at her. He did not. Lieutenant Collins offered her his arm and escorted her onto the dance floor where sets were forming up for the next dances.

* * * *

Travelling with the Quentin party Jonathan had arrived earlier than he would have chosen. They were greeted by the earl and countess and the gentlemen were introduced to their daughter, Lady Venetia. As Mrs. Quentin had the young lady's acquaintance and was anxious to speak to her father, who had also arrived early due to Lady Mary, Captain Quentin led his wife away, leaving Jonathan behind engaged in conversation with Lady Venetia.

"Sir Jonathan," she said, "I understand you have come lately from the Caribbean?"

"I have indeed," he replied.

"You must tell me what it is like, for I have heard stories of pirates and sea monsters." She fluttered her eyelashes at him.

"Pirates still roam the West Indies, Lady Venetia, but sea monsters?" He shook his head. "Exaggerated tales by those who wish to entertain and horrify."

"Oh, dear." She turned to her mother. "Mama, Sir Jonathan has promised to tell me all about the Caribbean, may I accompany him? It is so dreadfully tedious standing here being polite to people of whom I know little, nor wish to know better."

To his surprise, Lady Norton smiled condescendingly at her daughter, "By all means dear, Sir Jonathan will escort you, won't he?"

What could he say? No sooner had he stepped inside Penley Court than he felt like a pet spaniel, held on a tight rein by a young precocious lady who had taken possession of him by hanging onto his arm. He found his situation precarious.

"Let's go outside onto the terrace," she suggested.

"Lady Venetia, I do not know how young ladies are behaving in London at present, for I have not been into Society of late, but it was my understanding that young ladies do not allow gentlemen to escort them without a chaperone to places out of public view."

"Oh, you're as stuffy as my father," she moaned.

"Perhaps that is because your father, aunt, and I grew up together."

"But you're not as old as them, are you?"

Jonathan shook his head. "Not quite, your father is five years my senior and Lady Mary…it is not polite to discuss a lady's age."

"Oh, Sir Jonathan, let us not be so proper. I thought all naval officers in their dark blue uniforms were bang up to the mark."

Not entirely sure what she meant, Jonathan said, "Perhaps I should escort you back to your parents."

"If you insist upon it." She pouted. "but I would prefer to go outside onto the terrace."

"And I would prefer to take you back to your duty in the receiving line. Do not make a fuss, Lady Venetia, people are watching us."

He led her back to the entrance hall where her parents were greeting the long line of guests. He unhitched her hand from the crook of his arm, lifted her fingers to his lips and gently kissed her hand.

"Oh, how charming," she said, "and Mama, you'll be pleased to know I have just promised the first set to Sir Jonathan."

He narrowed his eyes as he looked at her, he disliked being forced into any position he had not chosen. What had motivated the girl to want to dance with him? And why the opening set of the evening when all eyes would be upon them? He nodded briefly to both ladies, eyeing Lady Venetia with annoyance. She was young, impudent and, if her parents did not act quickly to restrain her forward conduct, she would soon be totally out of control. He would dance with her, he conceded, but that would be the last he would have to do with her.

* * * *

Catherine passed a fairly pleasant evening, at least when she could suppress the way she felt about Sir Jonathan dancing with Lady Venetia. She danced two dances with Lieutenant Collins and scrutinized the ballroom for a glimpse of Sir Jonathan again. She saw Lady Venetia dancing with several partners, but not him.

In anticipation of the supper dance, she waited with Bella. Her heart soared when he arrived with Captain Quentin, took her hand, tucked it into the crook of his arm, and led her onto the dance floor. They were joined by several other couples to make up the set—including the Quentins. As the music struck up, the corner couples moved to the centre and formed a star. A series of turns and promenading followed, but no matter how many interchanges occurred between the set members, Catherine only had eyes for Sir Jonathan. Taller than most of the gentlemen in the set, except Captain Quentin, who was about the same height, Sir Jonathan looked resplendent, his gold epaulettes glistening beneath the flickering candlelight of the shimmering chandeliers.

Catherine closed her eyes momentarily to savour the scene. She had never felt happier. And when the dance brought them together and their gloved hands met, she marvelled at his gentle touch. His dark eyes, swept by his long eyelashes shone for her alone, or at least, she was convinced they did. The moment was magical, and she intended to keep it locked in her heart forever.

When the music stopped, they remained caught in each other's gaze, oblivious of the world around them. Catherine's elated feelings continued to soar, she was happy and cared little about the inevitable gossip that would follow over the next few days when every minute detail of the ball would be analysed by ladies at their sewing in the drawing rooms of Hampshire.

It pleased Catherine enormously as Sir Jonathan seemed determined to show her every courtesy when they entered the supper room. He found the choicest dishes and helped her to small portions; he also found her a seat at a corner table with the Quentins and a few other naval acquaintances. Their table must have borne a strong resemblance to a naval dinner with all the gentlemen in their best dress uniforms.. When Admiral and Lady Mary entered the room, Catherine expected them to go to the Norton's table, but, surprisingly, the admiral joined them.

"Can't let the service down, can I?" he said, his gold braid outranking all present. "No, no, be seated gentlemen." He waved his hand, then, looking at his wife, said, "Sit down Mary, the lieutenant can draw up another chair."

"The Nortons are expecting us," she said, "I've already accepted their invitation."

"Well I didn't accept and I'd rather choose my own company at supper. Sit down Mary, that's an order."

"If you put it that way, thank you Henry, I'd rather be here with you." She sat and the rest of the officers followed.

"Miss Ellis, I saw you dancing with Sir Jonathan and Lieutenant Collins," the admiral said, "I hope you are enjoying yourself?"

"Most definitely, Admiral Richmond. Penley Court is a most pleasant house and ideally suited for entertainment," Catherine replied.

"Good, pleased you think so, used to be Lady Mary's home, you know."

"Yes, sir, Mrs. Quentin told me so."

The conversation moved towards naval matters, especially talk of the poor state of the fleet and the

Peace. Catherine listened in silence. She was seated with her back to the wall next to Bella, with Sir Jonathan on her right, and had a good view of anyone entering the room. Most of the tables were full. Menservants dressed in the Norton livery brought in extra dishes of food.

Sir Jonathan was in deep discussion with several of the other officers, including the admiral, Lady Mary was talking to Bella, when Catherine looked up and saw Lady Venetia enter the room on the arm of a gentleman the exact likeness of her sketches. She grabbed Bella's hand. "Don't look now, but I believe a gentleman who looks exactly like your cousin has just walked in."

Bella did look. The colour drained from her face and she whispered something to Lady Mary, who also glanced in the gentleman's direction. Soon, Captain Quentin too had seen him, and nudged Sir Jonathan.

"What's the matter?" the admiral asked, his high forehead creasing.

"Granville is here," Bella said softly.

"What? Confound the impudence of the man," the admiral cried. "Mary have you got your pistol with you?"

"Hush, Henry, of course I haven't, this is a ball not a shooting gallery."

Heads turned in their direction. It wouldn't be long before their table attracted Mr. Richmond's attention. But why was he escorting Lady Venetia? Sir Jonathan's face looked stony, his breathing heavy, and his temper ready to erupt at any moment. Captain Quentin moved to restrain him.

"There's no need," he said shrugging off the captain's hand. "Apparently, you were right about flushing the fox from his den."

Chapter Twelve

Catherine awoke the following morning, leap out of bed, and threw back the curtains. Bright sunlight streamed into her bed chamber, it must have been mid-morning, far later than her usual rising hour. The small carriage stood in the stable yard below, and Mr. Winters' four horses poked their heads out of their stables, as if waiting for their daily tasks to be allotted to them. She turned away, moved across the room to ring for Martha, when the sound of a carriage turning into the yard brought her rushing to the window. It seemed an early hour to call, what time was it?

It was the Quentin carriage, driven by a coachman, postilion rider, and two mounted outriders, both armed with long muskets. The party looked formidable. Could it have something to do with Mr. Richmond at the Penley Ball? Much to her surprise, for she expected the carriage to carry either the captain or Bella, Sir Jonathan descended. She stepped back, covering her chest defensively, clad only in her nightgown, she felt vulnerable yet exhilarated to see him.

As he strode out of view, the door bell clanged, followed by voices from below. A tap on her door brought Martha within, her cheeks pinking, and her eyes wide. "Sir Jonathan has arrived. He is asking to see you, miss. His arrival has caused quite an upset. Mrs. Winters is running around with her hair still in rags, Mr. Winters and Mr. Ellis are at breakfast, and Mrs. Ellis is still abed."

"Quickly, get out my muslin with the pink ribbons, no...the green sprig...no, the pink," she said.

Martha opened the chest and unfolded each dress, placing them over her arms. She held her arms out wide, "Which do you want, miss?"

Catherine dithered. "The pink, yes the pink, don't you think?"

Martha discarded the other dress across a chair and set to work with Catherine's hair, untying the strips of cotton, letting her curls fall onto her shoulders.

"Something simple and do hurry," Catherine pleaded, her heart racing, her hopes rising. "Did he ask for me? What did he say?"

"I don't know, miss. I was passing through the hall and Sir Jonathan was invited to take breakfast with the gentlemen, but he declined. However, he did agree to sit with them until he could see you."

"Do you realise, this could mean...oh, I'm so excited. Papa did mention that Sir Jonathan had spoken to him, and Mama thought he was very dashing but after the ball last night, and when I saw him dancing with Lady Venetia, I felt quite jealous. And then when he danced with me, I could have flown to the stars, I was so happy. Then a certain gentleman appeared. He didn't speak to any of our party but his presence certainly cast a dark shadow over the whole proceedings. Do you remember the first time we walked through the village, we stopped by the green, near to the smithy and I sketched the coaches and people coming in and out?"

"Yes, miss, you taught me how to write my name and I was practising on my slate."

"Do you recall a rotund, pompous looking gentleman, medium height, light brown hair, fancy clothes?"

"The one with the high pointed collar?"

"Yes, he was the gentleman at the ball last night. He is Admiral Richmond's nephew but he is no longer received at Witton Abbey. Would you ask the servants, discreetly, you understand, what they know of Mr. Richmond?"

"Of course, miss."

Within ten minutes, Catherine was dressed, her hair arranged in curls on the back of her head with side curls pinned in place. Glancing in the mirror, she said, "Thank you Martha, I don't think I have ever looked better."

As she emerged from her bed chamber, she met her mother standing in her doorway, still in her night clothes. "I cannot come down, it will take too long for me to dress, but Sir Jonathan has come to ask for you. Catherine, he appears to be a very amicable gentleman, and he does have a title, but please, do not accept him if he is not the choice of your heart. You will always have a home with us, and your father will provide for you when he has gone. Only accept Sir Jonathan's proposal if you have deep affection in your heart for him, and him alone."

Catherine gently squeezed her mother's hands. "I love him, mother, I hope he loves me." She dropped a brief kiss on her mother's cheek.

As she descended the stairs, joy swelled in her heart. Was she truly going to hear his declaration of love for her? She took a deep breath, said a quick prayer, and went into the drawing room.

＊ ＊ ＊

Jonathan took at seat at the breakfast table but refused refreshment. Mr. Winters and Mr. Ellis were tucking into generous portions of ham and eggs.

"You came with a heavy escort, Sir Jonathan, for any particular reason?" Mr. Ellis asked.

Jonathan played down the issue. "Most of Captain Quentin's staff comprises his old crew members from the *Diana*, they are fighting men, sir, and need to train their skills. Whilst the captain cannot fire a broadside from the roof of Aston Grange, he can at least give his men escort duty."

"I like the cut of the captain's jib. I do not like to see men idle, very wise of Quentin. Although your escort could be construed as an armed guard, to ensure you don't change your mind on the way, eh?"

"Change his mind? What do you mean brother?" Mr. Winters asked.

Mr. Ellis smiled. "Sir Jonathan's come to make Catherine an offer, or at least I hope he has."

"Upon my word, I had not the slightest notion. Mrs. Winters said nothing."

"Because your wife doesn't know," Mr. Ellis said with a look of triumph on his face.

Jonathan kept his own counsel. Mr. Ellis obviously had the measure of his connections. A tap on the door brought Miss Ellis' maid into the room. She dropped a curtsy and waited for permission to speak.

"Yes," Mr. Winters said.

"Excuse me, sirs, Miss Ellis is waiting in the drawing room, I was told to tell Sir Jonathan she will see you now."

Jonathan stood up, nervous anticipation setting the hairs on the back of neck on end. "Thank you." He stood tall, swallowed, and strode out of the room in no doubt that his intentions would be the sole topic of conversation between the two gentlemen he left at table.

He paused at the door to the drawing room, tapped on the door, and entered. Miss Ellis stood by the window, the morning sunlight catching her dark mahogany hair. As she turned towards him, dropping a slight curtsy, her figure bathed in a glow of light, he thought she had never looked so lovely. "Good morning, Miss Ellis," he said.

"Good morning," she replied, "I hope you enjoyed the ball last night?"

He was pleased that she had opened the conversation, somehow it eased his tension. "Certainly the first half of the proceedings, until supper...I very much enjoyed dancing with you, Miss Ellis, in fact, I have delighted in your company since coming into Hampshire. From our first acquaintance, I have been taken with your kindly nature, good humour, and elegance of manners. In the short time I have had the privilege of your acquaintance, I have come to admire and love you. Miss Ellis, will you do me the honour of becoming my wife?"

"Oh, yes. Sir Jonathan, since we met I believe my feelings mirrored yours. Thank you. To be your wife would surely make me the happiest woman alive."

He stepped forward, took her hand in his, and gently lifted her fingers to his mouth, dropping the softest of kisses on the back of her hand. A combination of relief and joy burgeoned in his heart, he was to be married to a delightful woman—he could hardly believe his good fortune. "Miss Ellis, my dear Catherine, today you have given me hope for the future. Together we can only be stronger and face life's adversities in the firm knowledge of our devotion to each other."

Drawing her towards him, he looked deeply into her dark brown eyes and dropped a light kiss on her lips. Lifting his head slightly from hers, he said, "I am a man of action, I cannot wait long for our union, I have already spoken to your father. Let us be married at once, whilst your parents are in Hampshire. I can ride to Winchester and secure a licence from the Bishop. Listen to me, I speak with the impetuousness of a youth, eager to please and anxious to secure whatever happiness I can grab. Marry me, Catherine, marry me next week!"

"Very well, if my parents have no objections."

* * * *

The uproar caused at the parsonage by the news of the engagement was loud, especially from Mrs. Winters. After Mr. Ellis had congratulated the couple and Sir Jonathan had taken his leave, Mr. Ellis drew his daughter to one side. "I hope Sir Jonathan will make you happy, he is an honest and upright man, I like him immensely and shall be proud to have him as a son-in-law."

Her father's words pleased her, however, when he added that perhaps her wifely duties might prevent her pursuing her artistic ambitions, she couldn't agree with him, but didn't wish to argue when she was so happy about her engagement.

"I shall leave you now to your mother and aunt." He looked in Mr. Winters' direction. "I have persuaded Mr. Winters to take a turn around the village with me. I am interested in the workings of the mill and seeing the surrounding farm land.

"Oh! Mr. Winters," his wife leapt to her feet, "you do not mean to take the carriage? I have parish calls to make today, and might need to travel as far as Witton Abbey."

Mr. Winters looked at Mr. Ellis. "We can easily walk to the water mill and should the weather not hold, we could hire a curricle from the inn."

Mr. Ellis nodded his agreement. "Let us leave the ladies to their devices, brother." He turned to Mrs. Winters. "Spreading news around the neighbourhood can be very taxing, take the carriage. I'm sure you will find greater use for it today."

When the gentlemen had gone, Mrs. Winters wasted no time in organizing the ladies. "Catherine, send your maid to the kitchen, I have ordered cook to prepare a picnic basket for us, and there are two baskets of parish gifts. Your maid can accompany us and carry the heavy ones. Sister, you must ride next to me, Catherine and the maid can ride backwards. Come along, we have so much to do and a large number of calls to make. Come along ladies, make ready."

Elated, Catherine put on her bonnet and spencer, and climbed into the carriage. Martha was already inside, a large basket at her feet and another balanced on her lap.

Mrs. Winters knocked on the carriage roof for the driver and the small postilion rider to get them moving. The carriage lurched before moving forward at a steady pace. "Our first call will be to the farms along the turnpike road, then we shall go to Witton Abbey. I am sure we shall find Lady Mary at home, although she might have stayed over at Penley with her brother. Nevertheless, I can leave a message with the housekeeper."

Catherine cringed at her aunt's behaviour. But why let it dampen her joy? "Mama, I hope you are not feeling too tired after last night?"

"Do not worry about me," her mother said. "I am sorry we had to leave the ball so early on my account, particularly as you were enjoying yourself, but your father was fatigued too, however, he wouldn't care to admit it."

"I didn't mind quitting after supper," Aunt Winters said, "it was something of a crush, and I had spoken to as many of my acquaintances as I cared to. However, I did hear a rumour that Mr. Granville Richmond was in attendance. He is the admiral's nephew and something of a bad sort. Why, he caused the most embarrassing confusion by telling Mr. Winters and I that he was engaged to his cousin, when she had refused him. If he were at the ball, I'm glad I didn't see him."

They arrived at the first farmhouse. Mrs. Winters insisted on getting down and ordered Miss Cope to follow her with one of the large baskets. "Catherine, sister, do not trouble yourselves to descend, I have instructed the driver to turn the carriage and I shall only be a few minutes whilst I leave a few gifts for the children."

When Mrs. Ellis was alone with her daughter, she said, "I do wish my sister-in-law could restrain herself. She is like a bird constantly twittering. Does she not realize that few people listen?"

"Do not be too harsh on her, Mama, she has a good heart and her work around the parish supporting the poorer families is much to her credit. However, it is regrettable her main source of pleasure appears to be based on the amount of intelligence she can manage to circulate per day."

"Enough of your aunt. Has Sir Jonathan mentioned where you will be living when you are married?"

Catherine thought for a few moments. "I was so excited by his proposal, I gave no thought to my possible situation, but I suspect we shall settle at Westwood House, which is near to Droitwich Spa in Worcestershire. A few days ago, Bella happened to mention the place, she and the captain had been passing close by on their honeymoon and curiosity drew them to take a look at it. Unfortunately, the house has been closed up—Sir Humphrey preferred to live in town after his wife died—so Bella could not take a tour, but she did speak very favourably of the vista."

At that moment, Aunt Winters appeared at the carriage door and the driver assisted her inside, followed by Martha.

"Catherine, Mrs. Styles was delighted to hear your good news and sends her felicitations. She remembers Sir Jonathan very well from his boyhood, when the family spent their summers at Aston Grange, and hopes you will be very happy. She assumed you would be living there and I didn't tell her otherwise. However, where will you be settled?"

"Sir Jonathan didn't say, but I assume we shall be going to Westwood House."

"Of course." She smiled. "It must have slipped my mind. I'd forgotten Sir Jonathan intends to settle the mortgage with his prize money and the funds he receives on marriage from his mother's entailment."

Catherine sat up straight, "Aunt Winters, your knowledge of Sir Jonathan's business affairs appears very acute, might I ask how you came by this information?"

"From Mr. Winters direct, he has an uncanny manner of telling me all that befalls him during the day. I am so delighted Sir Jonathan is to acquire a Special Licence from the bishop and we are to have the wedding in the parish, and so soon. You must be very excited, to be married with such expediency, although under the circumstances, I thoroughly understand."

"Please Aunt Winters to what circumstances do you refer?"

"The late Lady Westwood's entailment, of course, if Sir Jonathan marries before Michaelmas he will have sufficient funds to settle the mortgage on Westwood House. It was extremely fortunate that the late Lady Westwood's father made a reserve, and a great pity he did not include the Aston Grange estate in the settlement, because if he had done so, Sir Humphrey would not have been able to gamble it away."

A huge black shadow descended over Catherine's thoughts. She sat in silence, closed her ears to her aunt's idle chatter and tried to make sense of what she had learned. Her mother said something, but her voice sounded yards away, not a couple of feet across a carriage. Was money the reason for Sir Jonathan's haste to marry? If so, would he have chosen the first suitable lady he thought might accept him without further inquiry? He said he admired and loved her, but Rossi had used similar words and he had deceived her. Her hand flew to her mouth and for one terrible moment she thought she might vomit. The bitter taste of bile welled up in her throat. She felt the colour drain from her face...

The carriage lurched, jostling the passengers from their seats. Catherine and Martha ended up on the floor. Loud cries came from outside. Aunt Winters stuck her head out of the window and screeched, "We're being robbed, highwaymen. Heaven help us!" She sank back into the carriage, her hands clasped together in prayer as she muttered the Lord's Prayer at speed.

Catherine got back into her seat and pulled Martha up by her arm. The carriage had stopped. A broad shouldered man, wearing a heavy boat cloak, tri-cornered hat and a kerchief tied around his face wrenched open the door.

"Get down, or I will fire!" He brandished a long duelling pistol in his hand, cocking the firing mechanism as he spoke.

"Quickly," Mrs. Ellis said, "we must do as they ask, our lives may depend upon it."

"You first," the highwayman grabbed Catherine's arm and pulled her out of the carriage. She glanced at the horses, they were being held by another of the brigands, whilst the driver and the small postilion rider were being tied to a tree by another of the gang.

The first highwayman stood on the carriage step, lent inside and dragged Martha out. He pushed her to the ground like a rag doll.

Catherine bent down to assist her. "Are you all right?"

Martha nodded, straightened her bonnet, and scrambled to her feet. "Yes, miss."

"Get out of the carriage," the highwayman shouted to the ladies inside.

Mrs. Ellis emerged next, terror etched onto her pale face. Mrs. Winters followed, protesting loudly.

"Shut your mouth," the masked man ordered, "or do you want to give me the pleasure of blowing your head off?" Mrs. Winters gasped, began to shake, and dropped to her knees. "Old hens are no use to us." He pointed his pistol at Catherine and Martha. "You two, back in the carriage."

Martha started to shake. "I'm afraid."

"Let's do as he says," Catherine said. She took the maid's hand and guided her back to the carriage door. They climbed inside. The highwayman produced a length of rope from his saddle bag, slammed the door shut, and tied a large knot around the door handle. He threw the rope to his compatriot on the other side of the carriage who secured the other door in a similar manner.

"They want us alive, keep that in your head. Keep calm, we must wait our chance." Catherine lent out of the window, to see the fate of her relatives. The carriage pulled away at speed, leaving her mother standing helplessly by the side of the road and her aunt wailing on her knees.

* * * *

"If you must ride to Winchester today, take Jackson and McCoy with you, I'll have them saddle Warrior. Do you think you can handle him?"

Jonathan nodded and was about to justify the urgency of his visit to the bishop when the doors burst open and Sanders and Jackson marched in with Mr. Winters' skinny stable boy sandwiched between them.

"Sorry, Captain, for the disturbance but this is grave news," Sanders said. "The parson's carriage has been held up along the turnpike road, highwaymen have made off with the carriage and Miss Ellis and her maid, Miss Cope inside. Mrs. Ellis and Mrs. Winters are shocked but unhurt, and the driver's got a sore head. This little mite ran to the nearest farm for help, then on to here." The men deposited the lad on the floor, where he crouched on all fours, gasping to get his breath back.

"By all the saints, it's happening again," Ross cried.

"Catherine?" Jonathan shouted, his anger erupting, his head reeling. "We must go after them."

"Turn out all the crew," Ross ordered, "Sanders send to Witton for extra men and horses. If those brigands take Miss Ellis the same route they took Bella, then we'll know where to find them. On second thoughts, Mr. Sanders, go to Witton yourself. Get written orders from the admiral, we might need his sloop if we have to pursue them across the Channel. Jonathan, we ride for Portsmouth harbour."

"What is going on?" Bella asked as she entered the drawing room, I heard the commotion upstairs, what's all the shouting about?"

As Ross quickly explained to his wife, she grimaced. Her hands flew to her mouth as if to suppress some deep-seated terror. Then she ran over to the boy and helped him to his feet. She spoke gently to him, asking for details about the men, how many, the arms they carried and how they spoke.

"Ross, I believe they are the same ones. The boy says they spoke with an accent he has not heard before and they wore heavy boat cloaks, tri-cornered hats, and carried long muskets. They've taken Catherine and her maid for the Barbary trade, haven't they?"

Ross put a comforting arm around his wife. "We do not know for sure, but the longer we stand around talking, the further they can get away from us. Go with Sanders to your father and stay there." He looked across at Jonathan, "We ride for Portsmouth and we shall have our revenge, I swear it!"

Jonathan's heart beat faster than it should. He wiped the sweat from his palms down his thighs. Catherine had been snatched from him. What if he lost her? He couldn't bear the pain he knew that would bring—she meant far more to him than he could possibly have anticipated.

* * * *

The carriage rattled along the road southwards, Catherine half-guessed they were bound for Portsmouth, but escape from a moving carriage meant either instant death from a pistol shot or broken bones. She would not wish either on her worst enemy. Leaning out of the window, she counted two masked riders. They stuck close to the vehicle as she heard the driver bring the whip up and unleash crack after crack on the horses' backs. She was no horsewoman but sensed the animals would soon be done for. One of the riders cried out to the driver in French, to ease the pace.

As the carriage slowed down, Catherine slipped back inside. "Those men are French, I believe they are the brigands who abduct young women like us and sell them into slavery on the Barbery Coast."

"Where's that?" Martha said, fear in her voice.

"North Africa. Women are sold in the markets as slaves and harem girls. Do not be afraid, they'll have to get us on board a ship, but they won't kill us, or worse despoil us. We are worth more to them alive and innocent. We must keep our heads. We have to find a way to escape. Our abduction won't go unnoticed. Sir Jonathan and Captain Quentin will come after us, but we must help them."

"I don't understand; how can we?" Martha cried.

"Leave a trail of clues, like in the fairy tales. Quickly, what do we have?" Martha hunted around the carriage, whilst Catherine leaned out of the other window to count the out riders again to confirm their number. When she returned to her seat, she removed her bonnet. "I counted four or five of them. I can't see if the driver has an assistant and there's only one horse tethered behind us. I'm going to throw this out, further along the way we'll get rid of the cushions and anything else we can use."

"Mrs. Winters' parish gifts and the picnic hamper?"

They passed other vehicles, but didn't dare lean out. The brigands were almost brushing the wheels of the carriage as they rode so close and had to duck to avoid the objects Catherine and Martha threw out periodically. Over the next quarter of an hour, Catherine and Martha deposited most of the carriage's contents, except the clothes on their backs, on the Portsmouth Road.

The vehicle slowed to a halt and the first masked man appeared at the window. "Stop your little trail game," he ordered. He untied the rope securing the door "Get out."

Slowly, they emerged, fearful of what might happen next. They were in the yard of an old farm, the buildings long abandoned, the thatched roof tumbled in. The man dismounted, drew a long piece of cord from his saddle bag, and bound their hands, whilst another rider looked on, brandishing his pistol in the air. Another man approached on foot with dirty lengths of sailcloth over his arm. The first man laughed loudly as he flung the canvas onto the ground, grabbed Martha, and forced her down upon it. She began kicking and screaming, but he slapped her face hard. Her hands went up to her head as she attempted to defend herself. The man showed her no mercy as he wrapped her inside the canvas sail and bound the rope around her body.

Catherine screamed at the top of her voice, hoping someone might hear her pleas. The brigand turned to her and flung the second piece of canvas over her head. Blackness and the musty smell of damp coupled with tar, filled her nostrils as the rope tightened around her body.

The man must have lifted her up. She was off her feet and struggling until she was flung, stomach down, onto the back of a horse. Another rope must have been used to tie her to the animal because she could hardly move as the horse walked on.

****

Jonathan rode with Ross and his men along the Portsmouth road at speed. They stopped to ask carters and other carriers if they had seen a carriage with outriders going south. The information was sketchy, but once they had recovered a ladies' bonnet and a basket similar to the one Mrs. Winters carried around the village, Jonathan was convinced they were on the right track.

"Captain," Jackson said, "there's an abandoned carriage over yonder in the clearing and a couple of spent horses."

They sped through the trees and dismounted at the Winters's carriage. Jonathan looked inside. "There's no evidence of foul play, except one of doors has been tied with rope."

"These horses look on their last legs, they must have gone on into Portsmouth on horseback." Ross said and turned to his men. "Make for the Point, we'll regroup at the Blue Post Inn."

Suffering an agonising mixture of emotions, Jonathan pounded the last few miles into the town. For the first time in his life, he had proposed to a lady, been accepted, and now, all his hopes for the future were being snatched away. Could Richmond really be behind this trouble? Had Catherine been deliberately targeted? Surely news of their engagement could not have spread so quickly to reach Richmond's ears, and what good would it accomplish to abduct her? He dismissed the idea of any conspiracy. He reckoned taking both Catherine and her maid had been a co-incidence. The brigands were searching for a few more young women to add to their cargo before they set sail.

He also was ashamed he had not taken Catherine into his confidence about his inheritance. He had been honest with Mr. Ellis, who seemed satisfied with his plan to save Westwood House, where he hoped they would settle. But now his future happiness was at stake, and the pain in his heart grew worse at the possibility that he might never see his love again.

＊ ＊ ＊ ＊

Catherine had no idea of where she was. The canvas covering her head and body stank of pitch and musty rope. She could hear voices, female voices whimpering and crying all around her. She had been hauled from the horse, slung over a man's shoulder and hit something hard. Her elbows ached, her knees smarted, and she thought she was going to be sick. Perhaps she had fainted.

"Is that you, miss?" a familiar voice said.

"Martha? Where are you? Are you hurt?" Catherine's head throbbed.

"I'm here, right next to you. I'm unharmed, I'm untying you."

The ropes loosened around her body. Martha pulled the foul smelling canvas away from her head. Gulping air and blinking, Catherine asked, "Where are we?"

"On a ship, I think, miss, and we're at sea, and we're not alone."

In the dim light from a single lantern swinging from the beam above, Catherine looked around and saw row upon row of young faces staring back at her. "All these girls. Where are we?"

"The lower deck of a ship, miss. Some of these girls have been kept here for weeks. They're all servants or farm girls. And they've all be taken like us, but I didn't have the heart to tell them what you said about going to that coast place."

The prospect of remaining imprisoned in the dark bowels of a ship was frightening, but Catherine didn't want to cause alarm. Any disturbance might bring their abductors down upon them. She had heard tales of slaves taken to America who had been jettisoned like cargo when the vessel ran into difficulties.

"Do not say anything until we know more about our situation. The men who abducted us, I believe they're French, but do not let them know I know their language, that way we might learn more of their plans. Tell me, what happened to you after we were slung over the carriage horses?"

"Some man pulled me off the horse and carted me over his shoulder, I pretended I had swooned and went limp. Next I remember struggling out of the sail canvas, my hands were still tied but I was in a damp cellar with half a dozen other girls. I searched frantically for you, but you weren't there. I was so worried about what they'd done to you or where they'd taken you."

Catherine reached for Martha's hand and squeezed it gently. "Thank you for your concern."

"I hated the cellar, especially as it was beginning to get dark outside. The last bit of light was coming in through an iron grating in the upper part of the wall. I stood on a barrel and managed to see out onto the quay, we was right down by the harbour. Then I felt something digging into my leg, I'd still got my slate in my petticoat pocket. I took it out and wrote a message on it. When night fell, the men came and carried us out one by one. When it was my turn, I played dead again. They picked me up and carried me across the quay to the ship, but before they could take me up the gangplank, I sprung to life and tried to make a run for it. They caught me, but not before I dropped my slate on the top of the harbour wall. I hope somebody finds it that can read and write, like me."

Catherine embraced Martha. "Oh, Martha, you have been most inventive, now we must be vigilant. What else we can do to further our escape?"

Chapter Thirteen

"Pleasure to see you again captain," the landlord said when Ross walked into the inn. "And Captain Westwood isn't it, sir, if my eyes don't deceive me?"

Jonathan acknowledged the man, ordered two glasses of brandy, and sat down at a table opposite Ross.

The landlord returned with the drinks. "Stew for your men, sirs, and ale?"

"Aye," Ross answered, "and information. Which merchant vessels sail for France on the tide?"

The landlord scratched his chin. "There's a few due out, trade's picking up a bit, wish I could say the same for the navy vessels. Let me see, the *Belle Marie* and the *Josephine* sailed this morning, and I did hear they were making the *Celeste* ready. She's a French brig, been in harbour a few weeks, but I don't know where she's bound."

There was a loud commotion at the door. Jackson and McCoy forced their way in frog-marching another man between them. "Excuse us, Captain, sir, do you remember this scrum Turner, who surfaced last time we was after those Frenchies? He claims he's been working for some English gentleman this time."

Ross stood up. "I remember you, so what do you know about the kidnapping of two young ladies earlier today, or do you need reminding again that kidnapping is a hanging offence?"

"Not guilty sir," Turner blurted out. "I never went with the Frenchies again, not after the beating you lot gave me. They've been around Pompey these past few weeks and I reckon they've been up to the same trade. But I ain't been helping them."

Jonathan rose from his seat, anger flaring through his veins, "You knew about this barbaric trade in white slaves and you stood by and did nothing!"

"Begging your pardon, sir, that ain't my business. The gentleman I work for says these girls are going to America. They ain't slaves they go willingly to be married to settlers in the New World."

Jonathan looked at Ross, then back at Turner. "Your employer, what's his name?"

"He's the Count of Alonso."

"And does he look like this?" Jonathan reached into his waistcoat pocket and pulled out one of Catherine's sketches of Richmond. He shoved it under Turner's nose.

"Aye, sir, that's him."

Ross grabbed Turner by his coat. "Where is he? When did you last see him?"

Turner coughed as he cowered down. "I ain't done anything wrong, I only see to the victualing of his ships, and pilots them in an out of harbour when needed. He went on board today, along with the girls bound for America."

Jonathan drew his pistol, cocked it, and said very calmly, "Which vessel, and if I think you are lying, I'll blow your head off."

The man quaked. "The count sailed on the *Celeste* bound for Cherbourg to pick up some French girls."

* * * *

Catherine woke as canvas was removed from the hold covers and light streamed in from above her head. Orders were given in French to let the girls out. They were to be allowed on deck for air, water, and food. She whispered to Martha, "Observe everything you can, we must be at sea, but we might still be in sight of the shore. Count how many sailors there are and if they are armed."

A rough hand grabbed Catherine by the shoulder and propelled her up the stair. As she emerged in the bright sunlight, she raised her hand to shade her eyes. She scanned the horizon, but there was no sight of land. Men hauled on a sheet, a foresail unfurled and filled with wind.

A young lad carried tankards of small ale to the group of girls, who grabbed them and drank. Catherine assumed, like her, they had not quenched their thirst since the previous day. She picked one up. The ale tasted bitter, but it moistened her throat and mouth. She was draining the last drops from her tankard when she spied a portly figure strolling on the quarter deck. He wore a dark tailed coat, cream pantaloons, and black felted hat, but what struck her most was his tall, high collar. At first, she could only see him in profile, but her heart began to pound.

He turned and faced her, his puffy cheeks overflowing the high points of his collar, his cravat cascading like a waterfall down his chest. It was the same gentleman she had drawn outside the inn in Aston, the same man she had drawn over a dozen times for Sir Jonathan, the same man who had escorted Lady Venetia into supper at the Penley ball—Mr. Granville Richmond.

She did not want to draw attention and stepped behind Martha. It was a mistake. She could feel his gaze upon her, and dearly wished she hadn't discarded her bonnet when they were in the carriage. Her gown and spencer distinguished her from the rest of the group. The girls wore dull country clothes and servants' aprons made of linen.

He lent towards another man, whom she assumed was the captain of the vessel, as he'd been shouting orders to the rest of the crew. Then Richmond was pointing at her. The captain barked another order in French. The men were to seize her and bring her below, 'the bit of muslin skirt' he called her. She turned to Martha and quickly explained that they were coming for her. "Do not do anything, pretend you do not know me, my life might depend upon it."

The maid looked aghast, her face creasing. "How can I?"

"You must remember, don't say anything, we shall find a way out of this. Sir Jonathan will not let us down, I know it."

* * * *

As dawn broke, the *Vesta* made sail. Mr. Sanders had joined the rest of the crew at the Blue Post Inn carrying with him Admiral Richmond's written authority to take the sloop to sea. Lieutenant Collins opened a new page on the log. "Who is in command sir?" he asked.

Jonathan looked up from the captain's table at Ross who was studying the charts. "I've resigned my commission I'd be content to sail under your command."

"Much appreciated, Jonathan, I'd be glad to have you as second officer. Mr. Collins, will you take the starboard guns, and Sir Jonathan larboard, Mr. Sanders will be sail master and post the crew to their stations. We're not fully manned, but with a fair wind, if I can't catch a French brig I don't deserve the half-pay I'm collecting."

Later, Jonathan stood with Ross on the quarter deck. The *Vesta* carried every ounce of sail she had and was making a fair speed. "It feels good to be at sea again, doesn't it, captain?"

"Aye, but I didn't think I'd be chasing a French merchantman again so soon," Ross replied. "When those villains took Bella, I'd have torn their throats out if I could have got my hands on them. But we sailed into a storm, the *Maria Claire* foundered, we didn't fire a shot. This time, there's more than one life at stake. He's got at least a dozen girls on board God knows what will happen to them."

"And Catherine?" Jonathan cried, "If he's harmed her in any way, I swear, Ross, I'll put him down like the dog. He showed my father no mercy and he'll get none from me."

"We need a plan, as soon as we sight the *Celeste*, with this westerly I'll ask Mr. Sanders to come up on her larboard side. Mr. Collins will have the starboard guns, which frees you for the boarding party. If she doesn't heave-to, and I expect she won't, I'll do my best to demast her. Then it is up to you and the boarding party to take her. I can't risk holing her, especially if they have those girls down on the orlop deck."

"She'll be flying French colours, what do we do about that?"

"Ignore them. This ship's a privateer. Admiral Richmond bought her from the Admiralty when she was decommissioned. I'll put up the Jolly Roger if it makes you feel better."

"Ah, I wasn't exactly planning life as a pirate, but I will go to the ends of the earth to get Catherine back."

Ross smiled. "I understand how you feel."

* * * *

"Come," a sailor snarled at Catherine and grabbed her arm. He forced her along the deck, opened the door below the quarter deck and pushed her inside, slamming the door behind her. A few moments later, the door opened again and Richmond walked in. He removed his hat and placed it on the table.

"Madam, I do not have your acquaintance, what is your name?" Richmond asked.

Catherine stood her ground and remained silent despite the tumult of emotion swirling inside her. She did not want to give him any advantage over her that he didn't already possess.

"Come now, I mean you no harm, you are obviously a lady of some consequence, your apparel, your demeanour."

"Why have I been brought here? Forced against my will aboard this vessel?"

"Captain Dubois believes you might be valuable to your father, for I see you are not married. Tell me your name, madam, and I will try to negotiate a suitable price for your release."

She didn't believe him for one moment, but was relieved he hadn't recognised her from the Penley ball. "Am I to believe that you, sir, whoever you may be, have nothing to do with the cargo of human life this vessel is carrying?"

"Of course not." He smiled, taking a lace trimmed handkerchief from his sleeve and dabbing his nose with it. "I am a gentleman, madam."

"Then what are you doing aboard this ship?"

"Simply taking passage to France." He walked around the table, flicked his tailed coat, and sat on the edge.

"So, we are bound for France."

"You are very observant, madam, now what is your name?"

"I could ask you the same question, sir."

A sharp knock on the door and the captain entered. His upper lip curled as his gaze ranged over Catherine. He turned to Richmond and asked in French if he could have the woman when he had finished with her.

Horrified, she tried not to react and struggled to keep her expression bland. Richmond, also speaking French, replied that he was sure she would prove valuable to them, and there were several other girls below he could have.

The captain sauntered over to the side cabinet, reached in, and brought out a decanter of red wine. He filled two pewter goblets, offered one to Richmond, and drank the entire contents of the other one He wiped his mouth with his sleeve and said that there was another ship coming up on them from the north-east.

Catherine's heart leapt. Could the vessel be a rescue ship?

"Captain Dubois would like you to have a goblet of wine, miss."

"No thank you, Captain Dubois," Catherine said, emphasising the man's name. He laughed loudly, turned and left.

Richmond moved over to the door, ensured it was closed, and stood in front of it. "Let me introduce myself, as there is no one of equal rank on board to attend to the formalities, I am the Count of Alonso."

"And I am the Queen of Sheba," she couldn't resist replying.

His face dropped, he took three strides towards her. She stepped back but there was no more room. He began to finger her dark tousled hair. "You are a very attractive female," he said.

"Leave me alone."

"No, I don't think so." He touched her shoulders.

"Take your hands off me."

He laughed. "I don't think you understand, your majesty, either you become more amenable, or I'm afraid your life is in great peril."

"Are you threatening me?" she asked determined not to succumb to his bullying. "Hardly the conduct expected of a gentleman."

"Let us say, I am using my persuasive skills to greatest advantage."

A loud boom rattled the ship. Catherine dived to the side of the cabin and crouched with her hands over her head. When she looked up again, Richmond had left. Frantically, she hunted for some object useable as defence. She opened the cabinet and found a box, which she wrenched open. A pair of duelling pistols lay inside, but she had no idea how to load them. She pulled one out of the box. It felt heavy in her hand. With great effort, she cocked the mechanism and pulled the trigger. The pistol clicked. She did the same with the other. They were useless as guns, but who would know? She cocked each one again and placed them on the table before her.

* * * *

"Heave to, merchantman *Celeste*," Mr. Sanders bellowed through the loud hailer.

"She's not answering, Captain," Mr. Collins shouted.

"Fire again, Mr. Collins, across her bows, if you please."

"Aye, Aye, Captain."

"She's manning her deck guns, Captain," Jonathan said. He crossed the quarterdeck, descended the ladder, and took the loud hailer from Mr. Sanders. He filled his lungs with air and bellowed the same order in French. Two shots flew through *Vesta's* sails.

"I'd like to give her a broadside, right now," Mr. Sanders said.

"Captain can't risk it, but it looks like we'll have to demast her to stop her," Jonathan said. "Have we got the small arms ready?"

"Aye, aye ,sir, all loaded and I've got my four best lads up top."

Jonathan raced back to the quarterdeck as the order was given to fire at the masts. The loud boom blocked out all other sound as *Vesta's* cannon fired, hitting their target, snapping both the French brigs' masts and bringing *Celeste's* topsails crashing to her deck.

Mr. Sanders gave the order to strike his mainsails, bringing *Vesta* alongside the demasted brig.

Now it was Jonathan's turn, using their grappling hooks the men got ropes across to the brig's rigging and began to scamper aboard.

The French sailors were ill-equipped for fighting—several were brought down on the deck by musket fire from *Vesta's* tops, and a few surrendered holding their arms aloft, pleading for mercy.

"Where is your Captain?" Jonathan demanded, when he got no answer he repeated the question in French. A sailor pointed to the cabin beneath the quarterdeck. Jonathan called for Jackson and McCoy to support him and edged his way towards the door. Cheers went up above him, as *Vesta's* crew overpowered the helmsman and gained control of the ship.

Armed with a pistol, Jonathan kicked open the door, and came face-to-face with his enemy. Richmond held Catherine in front of him, his hand over her mouth, and a pistol digging into her neck.

"Come any closer and I shall send her to meet her Maker."

Jonathan backed off and lowered his pistol. "You're cornered Richmond, how do you expect to escape?"

"There is always a way," he sneered, "she's my passage, as long as I've got her, a noble gentleman like yourself would never dream of shooting me."

Catherine struggled, but Richmond seemed to tighten his grip on her. The hairs rose on the back of Jonathan's neck. He couldn't let Richmond get away, but neither could he let him harm Catherine. He had to think of something fast. "How do you propose to get to the French coast?"

Richmond's chubby face widened as he scoffed, "Why, in my uncle's sloop, the *Vesta*, which I see you have kindly brought for my use. Bring Captain Dubois here."

Not letting Richmond or Catherine out of his sight, Jonathan called over his shoulder to Jackson, "Find Dubois."

"I want all the French crew and cargo transferred to the *Vesta*," Richmond demanded.

"You'll not get away with this, too many people can testify to your crimes."

"Then I shall have to ensure they do not live to do so, won't I?"

"You despicable cur, is there no end to your villainy? You had my father killed didn't you after you'd cheated him out of his estate? What had he ever done to you?"

"An old fool who was ripe for the picking, he deserved to have his land taken from him."

"And his life? So he couldn't accuse you of cheating? Is that how you deal with your victims. Is that how you plan to deal with us?"

Catherine struggled again, her muffled cries louder than before. Jonathan followed the movement of her eyes, she kept rolling them towards the duelling pistol lying cocked on the table and back at him. Panic surged through him like a maelstrom, surely she wasn't going to try to escape?

Jackson returned, pistol raised, and stepped through the door. "Dubois is dead and we've found two dozen girls locked in the orlop deck."

"Round up my men, "Richmond demanded, "or I'll kill her."

Catherine grabbed the barrel of the pistol with both hands, pulling it away from Richmond. A loud click, and then Jackson fired. Richmond fell back fatally wounded.

* * * *

Catherine blinked and she was in the comfort of Jonathan's arms. He held her tightly, dropping small feather-like kisses on her head. She clung to him, "I had to wait," she breathed heavily. "We needed to hear his confession, only then would we know this ordeal was truly over."

"Oh, my love, I thought I had lost you when you were kidnapped, I thought I'd never see you again," he said. "You were very brave, and utterly foolish. If Richmond's pistol hadn't misfired."

She brought her hands up to his chest and lifted her head from his shoulder. "I, too, have a confession to make. I knew the duelling pistol in his hand wasn't loaded. I checked them myself when I found them in the cabinet. The twin is lying over there on the table. Richmond picked one of them up when he returned. He must have come in here when he realised the ship was lost. Thank you for coming after me, I never gave up hope that you would rescue me." Her hand flew to her mouth. "Oh! Martha and the other girls, we must set them free."

"That's already been attended to, there is nothing more to worry about, except to board the *Vesta* and set sail for home."

If only that were true. He had said he loved her, and she knew he wouldn't go back on this promise to marry her. But her aunt's words about his inheritance returned to plague her, now that her kidnapping ordeal was over. Did he only wish to marry her to secure the mortgage on Westwood House? And with Richmond's demise, who would be the new owner of Aston Grange? Perhaps he wouldn't need a wife so quickly? Perhaps she should offer him an honourable way out of their engagement?

****

Several hours later Jonathan sat opposite Ross in the captain's cabin on board the *Vesta*. "What have you recorded in the ship's log?"

Ross spun the book around. "Read it."

Jonathan scanned the entry, stating day, date, position, time, and weather conditions. *Bore up and took possession of brig, found demasted and in need of assistance. Proved to be* Celeste, *laden with corn and general merchandise for Cherbourg, about 100 tons, 6 guns and 23 men. Have her in tow.* "What about the butcher's bill?" Jonathan asked.

"Six dead, nine wounded, including the French and Richmond. We'll be home by high tide tomorrow night if this westerly holds. I'm keeping the bodies in the orlop deck. I'd be content to bury the French at sea, but Richmond's body I must take back for the admiral. He'll want proof."

"Take them all back, if only to put the word around Pompey the Count of Alonso's vile trade is at an end," Jonathan said.

"And what of you? Will you be off to Winchester as soon as we get back to chase the bishop for one of his marriage licenses?"

Jonathan's face dropped. "I'd like to, but I've been feeling guilty about rushing Catherine. I haven't told her about the inheritance from my mother's entailment. I wouldn't like her to think I wanted to marry her just to secure the funds."

"Call me old-fashioned but finance is a man's business, you've discussed your affairs with Mr. Ellis, what more is there to say?"

Jonathan sighed. "I don't want Catherine to get the wrong idea into her head. You know how particular females can be. Once they've got a bee in their bonnet about something, nought will shift it."

"Then make a clean breast of it. Go, talk to her, there's little to be gained sitting here talking to me."

Jonathan rose to leave. "One thing Ross, would you stand as groomsman?"

"Just try and stop me." he smiled. "Now go and find her, have your chat, marry with a clear conscience, and don't be too long about it."

* * * *

Catherine stood at the ship's rail looking towards the horizon with Martha when Sir Jonathan approached. He looked so comfortable on board a ship, would he yearn for a life at sea again?

"Might we be private for a brief word?" he asked.

"Of course, Martha, could you go below and find the book I was reading?" The maid dropped a brief curtsy and left them alone. "We were taking the air. When will we sight the English coast?"

"Some while yet, we are making fair progress, but with the *Celeste* in tow, our homeward run will be slower." A muscle twitched in his jaw. "My dear, do you remember I said I hoped to acquire a Special Licence for our marriage?"

"Have you changed your mind?" Her stomach began to flutter, as if butterflies had taken to the wing. Did he want her to release him?

"No, I was about to ride to Winchester when we heard about the attack on the carriage. There is something I wish you to know. When I marry I shall come into part of my inheritance from my mother's entailment. I want to marry before Michaelmas to enable me to settle the outstanding mortgage on Westwood House. But Catherine, my love, when I was in danger of losing you, when you were snatched away from me and your life threatened, I realised how much you meant to me. If you wish to wait, then I shall have no objection, I love you and there is nothing I want more in this world than to marry you."

"Oh, Jonathan, almost from the first moment I saw you with my uncle in Portsmouth High Street I was drawn to you. I thought you would never notice me, and I wanted, so desperately, to be an artist. Now I want to be your wife more than anything else."

"But you must not give up your art; you have a rare talent, which can only develop as you mature. You don't have to give up painting to marry me."

Catherine's heart danced with joy, "I love you and would marry you tomorrow, but I doubt if we could get to Scotland in a day."

He laughed. "Even the fastest ship could not get us there. We shall have to be content with a Special Licence and your uncle conducting the service at Aston church."

* * * *

Mr. Winters had one service to perform in Aston church before the wedding of his niece and Sir Jonathan Westwood. The funeral of Mr. Granville Richmond was a solemn affair. Only the gentlemen attended, as was the custom. Admiral Richmond led the mourners, but had little to say about his nephew. Mr. Winters restricted his eulogy to readings from the scriptures rather than offering a long speech about the deceased. Richmond was buried in the churchyard with a plain wooden cross to mark his grave.

Catherine waited in the drawing room of Witton Abbey with the ladies for the carriages carrying the gentlemen to return, but as she listened to the conversation she doubted if there would be any mention of the deceased gentleman. Initially, she had worried about the fate of Captain Quentin's man ,Jackson. Would he be prosecuted for murder?

However, Jonathan had assured her that Jackson had shot in defence of her and would not be held culpable of murder. There only remained Mr. Richmond's business affairs, which the admiral had shouldered, although he was reported to have said, "Count of Alonso, bah. I'll not settle any debts accrued by him." And so, the ladies' conversation ranged over more parochial matters.

"Lady Mary," Mrs. Winters said, "I heard a very disturbing rumour yesterday that Lord and Lady Norton are quitting Penley, surely this cannot be true?"

"Unfortunately it is," Lady Mary replied, "I am most upset by it. My brother and his wife have made their decision and are entitled to do so, but it is their reason for leaving I find most disconcerting."

Mrs. Winters sat up, all ears, and asked, "And what could that possibly be?"

"Lady Norton has decided she does not like Penley. She said the house required too many improvements to make it comfortable. She prefers the Surrey estate." From her tone Catherine assumed that Lady Mary had little patience with her sister-in-law.

"Oh, my goodness," Mrs. Winters cried, "what possible improvements could she mean?"

"My sentiments exactly," Lady Mary said.

"So when will they be quitting the place, not too soon I hope?"

"By the end of next week, I understand, although Lady Norton is taking Lady Venetia and the other children to Surrey within the next few days. I feel bereft, just when I was looking forward to getting to know my nephews and nieces better, they are to be whisked away by their fickle mother."

"And Penley will stand vacant again, what a pity," Mrs. Winters sighed.

When the conversation cooled, Catherine was about to say something when Bella asked, "When do you plan to return to Lancashire, Mrs. Ellis?"

A serene-looking smile hovered on her mother's lips. It pleased Catherine to see her so content. "After the wedding, Mr. Ellis does not like to be away from his business for long periods of time. I fear he does not trust anyone else at the helm."

"Then our neighbourhood will be excessively depleted," Mrs. Winters said, "I was only saying to Mr. Winters this morning as he made ready for the service that we shall miss so many of our dear friends."

"That is the consequence of having a daughter married," Mrs. Ellis said to her sister-in-law, "I shall miss Catherine, but to have the pleasure of seeing a daughter well married, that is blessing in itself."

Middleton opened the doors and the sound of gentlemen's voices echoed from the hall. Admiral Richmond, as chief mourner, had led the cortege and entered first. He nodded to the ladies and sat down in his usual chair, resting his elbows on the arms, "I shall be glad when today is done," he said to Lady Mary.

"Indeed, Henry, but let us have closure and be restored by it."

He reached for her hand, "Wise words, Mary, as always."

Catherine's heart filled with joy as Jonathan entered, talking to Captain Quentin. Would she ever get used to the feeling of elation he was able to stir in her every time he entered a room where she was present? She would enjoy the emotion for as long as it lasted.

Mr. Ellis came in next, his white hair brushing the collar of his dark tailed coat. Catherine gave him a smile, although he could be a very blunt man, she knew he held her in great affection. She acknowledged him, rose, and offered him her chair next to her mother.

"Thank you, daughter," he said and sat down. Sir Jonathan and Captain Quentin took up position in front of the fireplace. A decorated fire screen stood in the hearth there being no need for a fire in August.

Admiral Richmond cleared his throat, "I have asked you all to gather here today because I wish to attempt to make some redress for the pain, suffering, and anguish caused by my nephew. I shall say nought of him, but my man of affairs in London says he made no will. As I am his heir, I shall attempt to settle his debts where the bargain struck was made in good faith. I speak largely of his tailor's bills and other tradespersons tallies. However, if, as he claimed, he did win Aston Grange from the late Sir Humphrey, then I now claim the house and land."

He paused to take a folded sheet of paper from inside his coat and held it aloft in his hand. "Here, Sir Jonathan, my written authority for transfer of the property. I return Aston Grange to its rightful owner."

Catherine saw awestruck amazement on Jonathan's face, followed by a beaming smile. He stepped forwards. "Admiral, sir, I do not know what to say."

"Take it, lad, it's rightfully yours." He waved the paper at him.

Catherine wasn't sure who started to applaud first, but soon they were all clapping their hands.

The door opened and Mr. Winters walked in. "Oh, my goodness, what have I done to receive such adulation?" he asked.

"Nothing," the admiral said, "you've missed hearing Aston Grange restored to its rightful owner. Fortunately, you are in time to toast the occasion with some of my best champagne. I liberated several cases of it from a French merchantman back in my post captain days. Middleton, pop open the bottles."

Whilst they were waiting for the sparkling wine to be served, Captain Quentin stepped forward. "I have an announcement, too, as Sir Jonathan will no doubt wish to take up residence, at least for the summer, my wife and I have decided to vacate Aston Grange. I have purchased Penley from Lord Norton."

"Oh, how wonderful," Catherine exclaimed as she joined the others in applauding once more. She turned to Bella. "We will be neighbours, I am so happy for you, for us all."

Mr. Ellis did not join in the applause but rose to his feet. A glass of champagne in his hand, he waited for the clapping to stop. "I wish to make a toast, to my soon to be son-in-law and my daughter. I admire a man who does what he thinks is right, who respects his friends, and does not ask a father the size of his daughter's dowry before he proposes to her. Sir Jonathan Westwood is an honest man; I hope he will accept a sum sufficient to settle the mortgage on Westwood House as a wedding present from myself and Mrs. Ellis. Ladies and gentlemen, I give you Captain Sir Jonathan Westwood."

About the Author

Lynda Dunwell is a LSE graduate and has taught economics and business studies for twenty years. She has worked as a press officer, advertisement copy writer and tourist information officer.

As a teenager Lynda read the novels of Jane Austen and Georgette Heyer. Today, she still dips into them to rekindle the flavour of the Regency life, which she adores including clothes, games, houses, pastimes and even food!

Although based in the landlocked English Midlands, Lynda loves the sea and adores cruising. She finds Regency history fascinating especially King George III's navy because there was a captaincy in every midshipman's tool bag.

She is a member of the UK Romantic Novelists' Association, the Historical Novels Society and the Jane Austen Society.

Lynda is a member of the Society of Genealogists and has traced her paternal family line back to 1485. Currently she is researching her female line which she describes as "far more challenging."

Website: http://www.lyndadunwell.com

If you have enjoyed reading Captain Westwood's Inheritance perhaps you might like the first book in this series about the families of Aston, Hampshire. Marrying the Admiral's Daughter is available from Amazon in print and ebook format